A MOST REBELLIOUS BRIDE

"You intend to go to York dressed like a groom and ride on race day? To be gaped at by every gentleman and country farmer alike?"

Moira's back straightened at his angry tone. "I do, sir, but you needn't worry—"

"I forbid it!"

"How dare you! You have no right to forbid me anything. I shall race Lucky and I shall win and there is nothing you can do or say—"

Without warning his hands were on her arms and he drew her to him. "Do you have any idea how dangerous such a race will be?"

Moira made a halfhearted attempt to pull away, but despite her anger at what he was saying, she liked the feel of his chest pressed against her. The sensations surging through her body made her struggle to put together her thoughts. "I can win. . . . I know I can."

His grip softened, and he lifted a hand up to trace the line of her jaw. "I suspect that you could, Moira. But they would never allow a woman to win a race. It would be a scandal. Besides, this is not some country contest. 'Tis one of the largest races in England. I couldn't bear it if you were hurt or killed."

With that, he lifted her chin and captured her mouth with his own. Moira was shocked at her own eager response to his lips. As a swirl of strange but wonderful new feelings surged through her, she realized she'd fallen in love with Lord Lamont. . . .

—from "The Scandalous Bride" by Lynn Collum

BOOK YOUR PLACE ON OUR WEBSITE AND MAKE THE READING CONNECTION!

We've created a customized website just for our very special readers, where you can get the inside scoop on everything that's going on with Zebra, Pinnacle and Kensington books.

When you come online, you'll have the exciting opportunity to:

- View covers of upcoming books

- Read sample chapters

- Learn about our future publishing schedule (listed by publication month *and author*)

- Find out when your favorite authors will be visiting a city near you

- Search for and order backlist books from our online catalog

- Check out author bios and background information

- Send e-mail to your favorite authors

- Meet the Kensington staff online

- Join us in weekly chats with authors, readers and other guests

- Get writing guidelines

- AND MUCH MORE!

Visit our website at
http://www.zebrabooks.com

ALL
DRESSED
IN WHITE

LYNN COLLUM
MONA GEDNEY
NANCY LAWRENCE

Zebra Books
Kensington Publishing Corp.

http://www.zebrabooks.com

ZEBRA BOOKS are published by

Kensington Publishing Corp.
850 Third Avenue
New York, NY 10022

First Printing: June, 1999
10 9 8 7 6 5 4 3 2 1

Printed in the United States of America

CONTENTS

THE SCANDALOUS BRIDE

LYNN COLLUM

CHAPTER ONE

"Sir, sir, wake up." The young maid shook the sleeping gentleman by the lapels, caring little about the damage she inflicted on his coat.

Mr. Sean Rourke stirred in the corner of the gently rocking carriage, not wishing to be disturbed from his dream of a lavish life in London after fortune had smiled on him. A sudden jarring bounce of the borrowed coach and young Doreen lost her grip, landing squarely in the gentleman's lap. Instinctively, his arms encircled the servant before she could scramble back to her feet. The Irishman, eyes still closed, nuzzled the feminine softness that had seemed to magically enter the real world from his imagination.

The maid wasn't discomposed in the least. Having spent her ten years of employment as Miss Moira O'Donnell's personal servant, Doreen was well acquainted with the lady's uncle and his philandering ways. Without batting an eyelash, she drew back her arm and planted an elbow in the gentleman's stomach, causing him not only to release her but to issue a loud groan as well.

At five and forty, Sean Rourke was still a handsome man, and rare was the occasion when a woman spurned his advances. Now fully awake, he eyed the maid with surprise as he rubbed his aching middle.

Doreen settled back in the seat opposite. ''There's no need to be givin' me that wounded sheep-eyed look. 'Tis sure I am we've no time for your foolishness, sir. Miss Moira's ill.''

The gentleman looked to where his niece sat slumped in the opposite corner of the carriage beside him. It appeared that Moira was in no travel-induced sleep. Her cheeks were flushed and an occasional shudder racked her body. Clearly the soaking they'd received as they'd arrived in England had given the girl a chill despite her assurances of being unharmed.

Fear gripped Sean's heart. He had been the one to convince his sister, Lady O'Donnell, that Moira's plan to travel from Ireland to England to race Eire's Luck was a good one. They had all been relying upon the fine Irish stallion, which trailed behind the carriage, to resolve their financial woes. It hadn't been easy to sway Edana to allow her daughter to go, but Sean had promised that he would protect Moira.

Illness had never been a part of his worries about their journey since so many other things might have gone wrong with the plan. He reached out his hand

and touched his niece's cheek. Her skin was hot and dry.

His hope was that the unseasonably warm May weather was responsible for the rosy flush, so he gently shook the girl. Her blue eyes opened, but the usual sparkle of enthusiasm was dulled by fever.

"Uncle Sean," she rasped out. "I fear I have ruined all our plans."

"Never you mind, lass. We've plenty of time to get you well before the race is run at York. Besides, there is Ascot soon to follow, and I've always had an urge to visit London."

Moira shook her head. "We haven't the money for such an extended stay in England. Everything was dependent on Lucky winning at Knavesmire Racing Grounds."

"Now, lass, don't be worrying about the money. Uncle Sean will take care of everything. First we must make certain you are well." He took her hand and patted it, wondering how he might be able to extend their funds if the horse didn't run as planned.

As his niece gave a wan smile and closed her eyes, the gentleman leaned forward and opened the window, shouting for the postboy to find a suitable inn for them in the next town. Sean hadn't a clue as to where they were since he never had been to England. He only knew that he had to get Moira in bed and summon a doctor. Without her calming influence on the highbred stallion, their dreams of winning the Gold Cup and then making a fortune by standing him at stud were worthless.

The carriage soon entered the ancient city of Warwick on Avon. Sean paid little heed to the beauty of St. Mary's spire, which towered above the city. Instead, he held his niece's hand and watched for a suitable lodging in which to safely settle her.

At last, in the middle of the small town, the vehicle pulled up in front of an old posting house called the Free Stone Inn. Shortly thereafter, Sean had Moira, with her maid in attendance, resting in a quiet room at the rear of the old hostelry. The physician summoned assured the Irishman his niece had a serious cold, but with proper care and rest would be recovered within a week or ten days. The doctor had no sooner departed than Moira wanted to arise and go see about the stabling for Eire's Luck.

"That you will not do, my dear." Sean pushed his niece back down on the pillow. He knew it would be difficult to convince Moira that he could manage things without her, for she was quite used to being in charge, having run the family estate since her father's death. "Why, are you thinking our Jim is flirting with a tavern wench and will forget to feed or brush or water our Lucky?"

Moira coughed before she lay back and smiled. "I have no worries about Jim. I do believe he loves the stallion as much as I. What if I should fall desperately ill or worse—"

"Close your eyes and rest. We have three weeks until the race and you will be long recovered by then. We can make the remainder of the journey to York in plenty of time. You mustn't worry over such matters or you won't get well. Doreen shall be here with you, and I shall be below stairs in the taproom if you need me."

Sean stood beside the bed as his niece seemed to accept his edict. His thoughts wandered to how he was going to amuse himself over the course of the week while his relative recovered. But then, to be honest, Sean Rourke had never had trouble finding something to amuse him wherever he was.

Moira's eyes fluttered shut as the sleeping draft the doctor had given her took effect. Sean urged Doreen to go to the kitchen and have something to eat before he left Moira in her care for the night.

While the maid was gone and Moira slept, Sean walked to the window and surveyed the rooftops of Warwick, for the inn sat high at the crest of a rise beside the River Avon. Since there were still several hours of daylight left, he decided that, after the maid's return, he would take a walk to see what amusements the town had to offer. As he turned back to the patient, Sean's gaze fell on the young lady's reticule, which lay abandoned on the table beside her bed. He picked up the bag and shoved it into the pocket of his coat, fearing that some chambermaid might come along and help herself to the money Moira had brought to finance their adventure.

Doreen soon returned and Sean wished her good night. He then set out to explore the town. After all, there was little he could do for Moira, and she wouldn't expect him to sit and mope while she recovered. She was a sensible girl.

He exited the inn yard and strolled down the narrow streets of the ancient city. He could see several watchtowers of the old castle they'd passed as they entered town, but since he'd never held an interest in antiquities, he veered left and made his way toward the river. When he could see the waterway at the end of the street, he came upon a large tavern called the Blue Whale. Filled with a desire to wash the road dust from his throat, he entered.

The tavern had a large taproom with high, raw-beamed ceiling. The room was filled with customers, mostly drinking, but what drew Sean's gaze was a table of men near the rear engaged in some kind of game. He made his way over and watched their play for several minutes. Listening to the gentlemen, Sean soon realized they were engaged in a high-stakes game of whist.

As the rubber ended, one of the gentlemen rose to the protests of the other players. He declared he had to return home, or his lady wife would be in a rare taking. When the others continued to object, he pointed at Sean, who was clearly a gentleman, as his replacement.

The Irishman remembered that he was holding the money for his niece. Here was an opportunity to increase their funds, for unlike the other men, his head was clear of the effects of drink. With a bow and little doubt about his skill, he accepted a seat at the table.

Life in Warwick proved to be surprisingly entertaining for Mr. Rourke during the week he remained. Each morning, he rose and breakfasted in his niece's room; then the day was spent with the group of gentlemen he'd met on his first night. Each afternoon, he would go to the inn stables and inspect their stallion, then return to again spend a few minutes with Moira, assuring her all was well with the animal before bidding her good night. On the evening of the eighth day, he returned to find his niece out of bed and declaring herself ready to resume their journey on the following day. Sean urged her to rest a few days longer for fear she might have a relapse, but she refused.

"We must get to York and find lodgings," she said. "Eire's Luck needs to be exercised before the big race." So Sean reluctantly agreed that they would again resume their journey on the following morning.

A few stars had begun to twinkle in the dusky sky as the curricle bowled through the village of Sherbourne at a shocking speed. Just beyond the town, a group of farm lads returning home from the fields were forced to scatter in all directions as the vehicle continued north heedless of all traffic.

Mr. Nigel Anson clutched his beaver hat with one hand and the side of the curricle with the other as he wondered what demon had gotten into his friend, Lord Lamont. Clearly, the private interview with his grandmother after nuncheon earlier that day had been the start of the gentleman's strange behavior, but he'd imparted no information to Nigel besides tersely announcing their departure from the Dower House at Fernbrook.

When the carriage hit a particularly large rut that nearly bounced Nigel from his seat, he decided to voice his concern. "I say, Colin, I didn't object when you got me out of my bed before noon to make this journey. And I didn't object when you rushed me away from Lady Ferries's table to return to the road. But I *shall* protest being thrown from your carriage to my death all in a fit of bad temper at your grandmama, for she shan't care a fig about my untimely demise."

Lord Lamont eyed his friend and traveling companion as if he had just remembered that the gentleman still accompanied him. The harsh lines in his face relaxed a bit, making him look more accessible if not exactly handsome. He eased up on the reins and allowed his team of perfectly matched grays to slow to a cooling walk. "Sorry, Nigel. I didn't mean to take my ill humor out on you or my cattle. You know what a dreadful temper I have."

"So I do." Nigel had been on the receiving end of a leveler from his friend during their days at Oxford over some trifling matter long since forgotten. "I take it the countess gave you bad news."

"The worst. She is demanding that I marry by the fifteenth of next month, or she shall end my allowance and settle her fortune elsewhere." The baron's pale brown eyes darkened with anger.

Nigel whistled softly. He, like much of Society, was well aware that Lord Lamont's late father had gambled away nearly everything save the small estate in Yorkshire, which had been entailed beyond his reach. The young baron was solely dependent on his maternal grandmother for his small income, and now the lady was using that as leverage to get her way.

"Why the rush?"

"I shall be five and thirty on that day, and she says all proper gentleman should be married by then. Says she wants to see I have an heir before she dies."

"What do you intend to do?" Nigel eyed his friend curiously. Colin was no weakling to be easily manipulated by his grandmother's machinations, nor was he a fool to whistle down a fortune rumored to be some fifty thousand pounds.

Lord Lamont's mouth pulled into a thin-lipped grin. "Oh, I shall do her bidding. I have little choice if I am to ever have any hope of returning Montmoorland to its former size and glory. But my grandmama will rue the day she issued her demand when she meets her new granddaughter-in-law."

Nigel arched a black brow as he gazed at his friend. Colin had never danced attendance on any female in particular in the course of the many Seasons he'd been in Town. In truth, he'd shown little interest in the social world, spending much more of his time in gentlemanly pursuits. Where the devil was he going to find a wife on such short notice? "You have a lady in mind?"

The baron nodded his head. "I shall marry the first scandalous lady who crosses my path. A madcap hoyden or an impertinent jade—it makes no difference as long as she is a lady born and bred."

Shocked to his very core, Nigel knew not what to say. "But . . . surely you cannot—"

Lord Lamont shook his head. "I can and I will. The matter is not open to discussion, my friend. Now shall we call it a day and find an inn in the next town?"

"Very well." The gentleman sank into silence as he stared ahead at the approaching town. There were any number of arguments against such a disastrous plan for a marriage, the first being that it was Colin, and not his grandmother, who was going to have to live with such a female. But in the heat of anger, his lordship was not likely to listen to reason. Nigel could only hope that after a proper meal and a good night's sleep Colin would recover his senses.

A knock sounded at Moira's chamber door the following morning. She called the visitor to enter as she finished pulling on her lace gloves in preparation for their departure from the Free Stone Inn.

Uncle Sean entered the room, and the look on his handsome face sent a shiver of fear down her spine. Her first thought was for her horse. "Is there something wrong with Lucky?"

The gentleman shrugged his shoulders. "Not exactly."

Doreen ceased packing clothes into a trunk to stare at the visitor, but the maid looked as baffled as her mistress. "Don't be sayin' the animal's taken ill, sir. He was a bit restless yesterday, but right as a trivet when I looked in on him for Miss Moira."

Uncle Sean sighed. "Don't be worrying about Lucky, lass. He's merry as a cricket. The problem is with the landlord of the Free Stone Inn and payment of the shot."

Moira nodded, then began to look for her blue tatted bag, which was the same hue as her traveling gown. She chided herself for having forgotten all about the money she'd scraped together for their trip. "Tell him I shall be with him shortly. Doreen, have you seen my reticule?"

The maid disavowed having seen the article since their arrival, then set about searching the drawers of the nightstand beside the bed. But before Moira could do the same with the small cupboard against the wall, Sean Rourke cleared his throat. His arm was extended towards his niece, the reticule hanging thin and deflated at the end of its drawstring.

"I took it into safekeeping on the night of your arrival."

Moira's gaze was riveted on the bag. She knew at once that a great many, if not all, of the banknotes she'd brought were now missing. In a voice barely above a whisper, she asked, "What have you done, uncle?"

"Lass, I . . . that is . . ." The gentleman hung his head in shame. "Thought I could get us out of low tide in case we didn't make York in time. And I was up fifty pounds, that is, until last night. Lost it all."

It was fortunate for Moira that the bed was beside her, for she nearly swooned at the news of their financial ruin. Everything she had been working for during the past two years had been lost by the turn of a card. There they were, in the middle of England in a carriage they'd borrowed from Uncle Sean's old friend in Bristol, with little or no money for food, lodging, or even another postboy and team to get them either to York or back to Bristol.

Her bleak blue eyes gazed at her relation with disbelief. "How could you do such a thing, Uncle Sean?"

But before the gentleman could explain, a sharp knock sounded at the door. The Irishman opened it and a very saucy chambermaid eyed the trio with disdain. "Mr. Stiller is wishin' to see the lot of you in the taproom this very instant."

Moira's stomach clenched in a tight knot. Whatever were they going to do? No doubt, in such a small town, the innkeeper knew of her uncle's losses. He would demand payment, since they had announced their departure to him the following evening. Then she remembered the valuable set of silver brushes in her vanity case, one of the few remaining treasures from her father. She rose and smoothed the blue cambric muslin of her simple traveling gown.

"Doreen, please bring my bandbox." With that, she swept past her uncle without a word and marched down the stairs and into the taproom. She paid scant heed to the other travelers, who were breakfasting. Instead, she walked straight up to Mr. Stiller, a stout, florid fellow with a malevolent look on his countenance and not a single hair on his shiny head.

"Sir, you wished to speak with me."

"Speech ain't what I'm wishin' for Miss O'Donnell." He pull a sheet of paper from the counter behind him and handed it to the young lady. "Nine days of lodgin' and meals for four plus grain for that fine steed in the stables. I'll be wantin' my money or some compensation for such an expense, or I'll be callin' the magistrate. I know you're rolled up, for I heard the gent was cleaned out last evening at the Blue Whale."

Moira's knees began to shake. "Sir, there is no need for such drastic action. I promise we shall pay, but first I must go—"

"You ain't goin' anywhere, miss. Not till I see the coin for this bill." He shook the paper in her face.

"Sir, I am on my way to York to race Eire's Luck at Knavesmire for the Gold Cup in two weeks. Can I not leave something of value with you to hold until he wins? Then I shall return and redeem it with coin."

"*You* shall enter that horse in a race." Mr. Stiller's voice was so loud and full of disdain that the few occupants of the taproom all looked curiously at the pair before returning to their meals. "What kind of proper lady involves herself with the Fancy?"

Things were not going well, but Moira lifted her chin with dignity. "Sir, I do not have to explain myself to an innkeeper. As to that horse, I do assure you he shall be the next star of the racing world. If you will but—"

"Fast, is he?" Mr. Stiller's small eyes narrowed. "That is as may be, miss. But that animal ain't leavin' Warwick till your shot is paid in full. He remains in my stables till then."

Moria stood speechless, horrified at the thought of losing her beloved Lucky even if only temporarily. But Uncle Sean, who'd been standing quietly, allowing his niece her say, entered the argument.

"Sir, you are speaking to Sir Curran O'Donnell's daughter, of O'Donnell Farm near Cork. You cannot keep my niece's horse. She needs the animal to get you your money."

A nasty grin settle on the innkeeper's face. "I can and will keep your galloper until I get my blunt."

Across the taproom, Colin Reed, tenth Baron Lamont, had been enjoying a hardy breakfast of steak and ale with Nigel Anson. The baron had spied the young lady the instant she'd entered the public room with her maid, and he'd recognized the lady as a genteel female.

Colin surveyed her with interest as she stood in heated conversation with the innkeeper. She was small, even by female standards, barely topping five foot, but she displayed an elegant figure in her unfashionable blue traveling gown. Her reddish-blond hair was neatly pulled into a tight chignon at her neck, but its natural curl resisted the constraint, leaving a few tiny ringlets nestled around her lovely oval face. Wide blue eyes were fringed with dark lashes and her full mouth was drawn into a downward arc as she listened to Stiller's threats.

Since Colin was unable to avoid hearing the content of the argument, it was clear to him that the Irish lady and her uncle were newly arrived in England and soon to race an animal in York—*if* they could wrestle the animal away from the determined innkeeper. But clearly something had gone wrong and the pair were purse pinched in some dire manner.

While Colin listened to the lady and her uncle try to bargain with a pair of silver brushes for the payment of their bill, Colin realized they were likely a pair of penniless adventurers. Then he paused. The man had mentioned Cork.

An Irish adventuress. The seed once planted grew into an outrageous idea. When the full plan came to him, Colin laughed aloud, causing Nigel to pause before taking another bite of his eggs.

"Well, I am glad to see you are in better spirits this fine morning." His lordship's mood made Mr. Anson hope that his friend had given up the preposterous plan of marrying some scandalous female to spite his grandmother.

Colin leaned back in his chair, his amber eyes twinkling at his companion. "Yes, there is nothing like a good night's sleep to clear the mind. By the by, did I ever tell you that my dear grandmother was once briefly married before she met the late Earl of Ferries."

Mr. Anson looked at Lord Lamont with little curiosity and instead wondered if the landlord was ever going to finish with his shabby customers and get around to sending for the second round of ale Colin had ordered earlier. "I don't believe so."

"Well, she was. She was quite young and foolishly imagined herself in love. But alas he died riding to the hounds."

"Is that where her personal fortune is derived?" In truth, Nigel had little interest in his friend's private affairs, but he asked his question out of politeness since the gentleman seemed determined to discuss the countess.

Colin chuckled. "Heavens, no. All dear Grandmama got from that marriage was an intense dislike of all things Irish, for the gentleman was from Dublin—a fact that is about to play very much to my advantage.''

As the baron rose, Nigel frowned, not taking his friend's meaning. Then his eyes widened in horror as he watched the young lord join the disreputable group surrounding the landlord. Colin bowed before a female who was decidedly pretty, but certainly not the thing. No respectable female would engage herself in a very public argument.

Nigel wondered if his worst fears were about to be realized. Colin seemed intent on making good on his threat to wed merely to displease Lady Ferries. Did his friend plan to marry this penniless Irish chit he'd found in a Warwickshire inn? The thought left the young man at the table frozen in horror.

CHAPTER TWO

Moira was at her wit's end. The innkeeper was adamant about keeping Eire's Luck until he got his money. Unfortunately, thanks to Uncle Sean, they no longer had any money to give him. She'd offered him the one thing of value she still possessed, but he'd refused the silver brushes, declaring he was no pawnbroker and would take only money. Even her uncle had gotten into the fray, and still the landlord could not be dissuaded from his determination to keep their horse.

"Ah, Mr. Stiller," a deep masculine voice said, interrupting Moira's thoughts.

The innkeeper was suddenly all politeness as he turned to the man who joined them. "My lord, what can I do for you?"

Moira looked to see a gentleman smiling at her

with a rather predatory gleam in his pale brown eyes. He wasn't handsome in the classical sense. His nose looked as if it might have been broken at some earlier time and his forehead was a trifle high, but his friendly smile gave him a definite appeal.

"Perhaps I might be of some assistance to"—he looked straight at Moira with a questioning arch of a brown brow—"was it Miss O'Donnell?"

After Moira nodded her head mutely, the stranger nodded to the innkeeper. "If you would give me a moment alone with this lady and gentleman, my dear sir, I think we might work out some arrangement that will prove satisfactory to both you and your guests."

Mr. Stiller frowned, but reluctantly agreed. He moved behind the counter, never taking his eyes from the pair who owed him money.

Uncle Sean, sensing something untoward in the works, stepped between Moira and the man who'd intruded into their affairs. "Now see here, sir. I'll not have you making any improper proposals to my niece just because we find ourselves at points nonplus. The lass is the daughter of a baronet, sir, not some common baggage."

His lordship laughed. "Sir, you mistake the matter. I do have a proposal in mind but nothing to make you or the young lady take offense."

Moira eyed the man with curiosity. "What proposal, sir?"

The gentleman looked about him, then gestured toward an empty table in the corner. "Shall we have a seat where we might converse more privately?"

Moira followed her uncle and the stranger to the

table, where she sat on the edge of the chair, her back rigid with tension. Despite the stranger's assurances, she was wary of the gentleman offering help.

His lordship took a seat after introducing himself, then gave Moira a winning smile that made her feel strange in the pit of her stomach.

"I hope you will forgive me, but I fear I overheard your conversation. No doubt all in the taproom are aware of your desperate situation."

Moira blushed. She couldn't bring herself to look at the other people in the room, knowing that they either disdained her situation or pitied her. "I must apologize for such an unseemly scene, but circumstances—"

"No need, Miss O'Donnell. But from your conversation, I understand you have a remarkable horse that you intend to take to the races in York."

Moira smiled with pride. "Eire's Luck, sir. I think he would rival the famous Eclipse, were that champion still alive."

Lord Lamont nodded his head. "No doubt. But unless you can get him to York, he cannot dazzle the sporting world."

Moira leaned forward as she realized the titled man might hold some sway over the innkeeper. "Can you not convince Mr. Stiller that my silver brushes are worth enough to cover our lodging? Then he will let Lucky go."

His lordship looked over at the bald innkeeper and grinned. "I think that gentleman's need for brushes is long past."

Moira couldn't help but laugh. "Don't be absurd,

sir. 'Tis the silver that is of value, not the brushes themselves.''

"I think that your horse is the solution to your problem, not your brushes, Miss O'Donnell.''

Suddenly Moira was struck with the direction the conversation was heading. "Eire's Luck is not for sale, sir.''

"Nor am I offering to buy him. What I am offering is to pay your shot here at the Free Stone Inn and to offer my estate in York as lodging for you and your uncle. There you can exercise the horse to ready him for the big race." Lord Lamont glanced from Miss O'Donnell to her uncle as he finished his suggestion.

Sean Rourke sank lower in his chair, knowing there was some catch to such seemingly good fortune. "In exchange for what, my lord?''

"For a third of the horse's earnings both on the track and off.''

Moira's initial reaction was to say no. Eire's Luck had been her family's hope for restoring O'Donnell Farm's financial security. She had a mother and two sisters in Ireland still struggling to make ends meet from day to day as they awaited her success. She'd thought it only proper to give Uncle Sean a third share in the horse for coming with her and acting as her protector. How could she afford to give up another third of the valuable animal?

Sean watched the play of emotions on his niece's face. He knew what was going through her mind, but he also knew that, if they didn't reach York in time to race the stallion, all their dreams and plans were for naught. "My dear, I would suggest you take Lord

Lamont's offer. A third of a winning purse is far better than two thirds of nothing."

Moira knew he was right, but still she hesitated. There was something in his lordship's amber eyes that disturbed her. She felt as if she were a sparrow under the menacing gaze of a hungry cat. Then she told herself she was being ridiculous. After all, Lord Lamont had been a perfect gentleman and Uncle Sean was there to protect her.

"Very well, my lord. We accept your generous offer."

The gentleman gave them directions to his estate, Montmoorland. After bidding them a safe journey, he went to settle the bill with Mr. Stiller.

Moira watched Lord Lamont closely as he paid their shot, wondering what his motive was for wishing to be part owner of a racehorse. He joined another gentleman, then exited the taproom with a polite bow to them. She suspected that a winning purse had little to do with his helping them. But at the moment, his true reason for involving himself in their affairs escaped her.

She looked over at her uncle, who seemed equally lost in thought. "We shall have to find someplace to sell these brushes in order to hire a new team and postboy."

Sean Rourke rose, offering his arm to his niece. "Come. I know where we can get an excellent price for them." As he led her from the inn, he added, "We were most fortunate to have encountered his lordship in our hour of need."

"That, dear uncle, remains to be seen."

* * *

Montmoorland was a large redbrick Tudor manor
built by the first Baron Lamont during the reign of
Queen Mary in the sixteenth century. Two wings that
formed a U-shaped courtyard had been added some
hundred years later when the family fortunes were
still on the rise. But for the past fifty years, little money
had been expended on the structure and grounds,
and the majestic building showed signs of neglect.

On the afternoon following the scene in the taproom, their carriage rolled up the weed-infested drive
of Lord Lamont's estate. Moira stared out the windows in surprise. Somehow she had not expected to
find his lordship's circumstances in such dire straits
as the property indicated. Yet she felt a sense of relief
as she gazed across the overgrown lawns at the clutter
of dead limbs and leaves lying about. The gentleman's
motives were much the same as their own and not
nefarious as she had feared.

Uncle Sean leaned forward to get a better look at
the manor. "To be sure, this will be a great deal more
comfortable than some noisy inn in York."

"Since it is costing us a third share of Lucky, I
should hope it will be comfortable."

There was no bitterness in Moira's tone. Still Sean
slumped back in the seat and looked sheepishly at
his niece. "My dear, I feel that, since I am responsible
for our being in this position, perhaps I should give
back my share of the stallion."

Moira drew her gaze from the great house. With a
kind smile, she said, "Despite your faulty judgment

in Warwick, I could not have come this far without you, dear sir. I insist that you remain a partner."

Sean sighed with relief as the postboy drew the carriage into the courtyard at Montmoorland. His pockets had been to let for years and Moira's scheme to race Eire's Luck had been a godsend. He would have hated to think his lapse in judgment had cost him his best chance for financial security.

The carriage had scarcely halted when Lord Lamont himself opened the weathered oak door and stepped out to greet his guests. "Welcome to Montmoorland, Miss O'Donnell, Mr. Rourke. Allow me to introduce my friend, Mr. Nigel Anson."

Moira stepped down from the coach, then took note of the man standing behind Lord Lamont. The gentleman was slightly shorter than his lordship with a handsome face and an arrogant set to his thin lips. The stranger's mint green coat with honey colored buckskins far outshone Lord Lamont's plain black superfine, which was worn over gray buckskins. But what struck her most was the look in Mr. Anson's dark eyes. Why, his lordship's friend almost seemed to pity her.

That was one thing Moira had never tolerated, even in Ireland when her family had been so desperate after her father's death. She straightened her back as she gave the gentleman her hand in greeting. She would show him there was no need to pity her. She turned to Lord Lamont. "My lord, I should like to accompany Jim and Eire's Luck to your stables to make certain all is to my liking."

"Shall we all go?" His lordship didn't wait for a

reply. Instead, he led the way to the rear of the coach, where Jim, the groom, stood with a magnificent chestnut stallion with a white star on his face and a single white sock on his front leg. As the group of admirers gathered round, the horse grew restive and began to dance and pull against the lead rope. Moira stepped forward and began to stroke the animal's neck while she crooned calming words. Eire's Luck became quiet, then brushed his head against the small young lady and grew almost docile.

Mr. Anson raised his quizzing glass to inspect the animal.

"He's magnificent, Miss O'Donnell. Where did you find such a fine creature?"

"My late father bred him and we trained him right on our farm." Moira glanced from Mr. Anson, who was closely inspecting the points of the horse, to Lord Lamont, who appeared to be giving her an equally intense perusal.

When his lordship's gaze met hers, he gave Moira an engaging smile, which suddenly made her feel quite weak in the knees. "How many races has he won?" he asked.

She suddenly found it difficult to concentrate. "Why . . . I believe . . . four in Ireland."

"Then I made a very wise move to invest in this . . . fine animal." The gentleman's gaze flicked only briefly to the horse before returning to Moira.

Mr. Anson allowed his quizzing glass to drop. "Well, I will most certainly wager on him, for I always put my blunt on animals with a single white sock."

Uncle Sean chuckled. "Aye, I see you've heard the Irish saying that one white sock is lucky."

The gentleman looked down his nose at Mr. Rourke. "Irish, indeed. 'Tis an ancient Saxon saying, old fellow."

Moira, realizing the gentlemen were about to bandy words about the old superstition, looked at Lord Lamont. "I should like to get Lucky settled in his new home before we dine, sir."

Lord Lamont led them to the stables, which sat some distance from the house. The redbrick structure appeared nearly abandoned, with its paddocks full of weeds and one of the large doors hanging slightly askew. When they entered the building, his lordship called, "Higgins, where are you?"

His voice echoed in the nearly empty stable, but the only response was the nicker of one of the grays whose heads protruded from their stalls. Then the sound of running feet could be heard and a lad who barely looked seven entered the stable.

He halted nervously in front of Lord Lamont. "Me Da's injured, my lord. Says I'm big enouf to be doin' the feedin' and muckin'."

His lordship frowned and Moira thought he was going to yell at the young boy, but instead he kindly inquired, "Will, what happened to your father? Has the doctor been sent for?"

"Da was climbin' into the loft, sir. A rotted rung on that ladder"—the lad pointed to steps that disappeared into the ceiling of the stable—"done give way and down he come. Keeps sayin' he won't have no

sawbones in the house, but his leg looks right funny
to me, all swelled and purple, sir.''

Lord Lamont shook his head. ''Your father's fear
of doctors will likely get him killed someday, my boy.
His injury should be looked at by someone who has
some skill with medicine.''

The lad merely nodded, before adding, ''When Ma
were alive, she done all the takin' care of us that was
needed. Now there's no one.''

Moira could see the young boy was worried about
his father. ''My lord, I have often helped my mother
care for the workers at O'Donnell Farm. Perhaps
Higgins will let me take a look at his injured limb?''

It was clear by the upward quirk of the gentleman's
brows that he was surprised at her offer. ''Should you
have the skill, Miss O'Donnell, I'm certain Higgins
wouldn't object to the tender mercies of a lady.''

With businesslike efficiency, Moira gave her groom
instructions on where to house Eire's Luck and how
much grain and hay to feed the tired animal. Then
she followed young Will away to the cottage of the
head groom of Montmoorland.

By the time she returned, her stallion was contentedly munching on hay in an end box. The two
Englishmen were questioning the Irishman on the
animal's racing history.

As Moira entered the building, Sean Rourke
seemed relieved. ''You were gone for an age, child.''

''How is Higgins, Miss O'Donnell?'' the earl
inquired.

''You will be pleased to hear that his ankle is only
sprained, my lord. But I assured him that our Jim

could easily take care of Eire's Luck as well as your horses and that he was not to get out of bed for at least a week. Will said he would make certain his father followed my instructions."

Moira felt positively breathless when Lord Lamont smiled and stepped forward, offering her his arm. "Well done, Miss O'Donnell. Now shall I escort you to the manor, where my housekeeper will show you to your room? I understand all young ladies like to rest before dining. Now that you are at Montmoorland, you must allow the gentlemen to handle all the matters with Eire's Luck and the race. No need to worry your pretty head over such things."

Uncle Sean snorted, then coughed when his niece frowned at him. "Moira might need a rest, but I could use a good drink. Would you be having any Irish whiskey, my lord?"

Nigel Anson, who fell into step behind the departing Miss O'Donnell and his lordship, remarked over his shoulder, "The only *civilized* drink before dining is sherry, sir."

Uncle Sean looked at Jim and rolled his eyes. In a low voice, the Irishman said, " 'Twill be luck for sure, if I don't murder one of these stiff-as-starch Englishmen before the race, laddie." With a wink at the laughing groom, Mr. Sean Rourke strolled after the departing trio.

Lord Lamont stood before the open double doors of his library. A glass of brandy in his hand he stared at the moonlit garden beyond the terrace. The night air was still and warm, leaving Colin with little desire to seek his bed. His thoughts were not on the overgrown lawns or the unkempt shrubs before him, but on the charming lady with whom he'd dined that evening.

Miss Moira O'Donnell was something of a puzzle to him. She knew a great deal more about the world of racing than any properly bred female should. Yet she'd handled Higgins's injury like any lady to the manor born. Her conduct during dinner that evening would have been acceptable to the highest stickler in Society, except when the subject of racing had again become the topic. Then she'd exhibit far too much interest and knowledge on the subject. Was she an adventurer as he'd surmised or merely an eccentric provincial?

His thoughts interrupted by the sound of the library door opening, Colin turned to see Nigel enter the room. He seemed slightly on the go, but then that didn't surprise Colin. The gentleman had been trying to drink Sean Rourke under the table since the covers had been removed and Miss O'Donnell had retired to her room.

"You are going to have a dreadful head in the morning, my friend."

Nigel waved a dismissive hand, then found he needed it to steady himself on a nearby chair. "Was worth it to prove to that Bog Trotter I can handle strong spirits as well as any man."

"Shall I ring for Larkin to help you to your room?" As he watched his friend sway, Colin doubted the drunken fellow could make it up the stairs by himself, much less find the proper door to his chamber.

"Not yet. Have something important to say before I retire." With bloodshot eyes, Nigel gazed blearily at his friend for a moment. "I wouldn't give you a farthing for that old rascal Rourke. Truth is, I'm as certain as I'm foxed he's an adventurer, a loose fish, but that niece is another matter. A lady of quality without a doubt. I know you're in high dudgeon at Lady Ferries, but are you willing to draw an innocent young lady into your game of revenge? Always knew you to be hot tempered but never cruel."

Colin walked to the bell-pull and yanked angrily. "You need to go to bed, Nigel. Larkin will escort you. In the future, I would kindly suggest that you refrain from interfering in matters that are none of your business."

"Dash it, Colin. I've a mind to lock you in your room till you come to your senses."

Colin gave a sudden laugh. "You must be quite serious if you would risk your life in such a manner." He paused and eyed his drunken friend for a moment, then added, "I promise I shall give the matter its due consideration before I come to a decision."

When the aged butler arrived, Nigel accompanied him without protest. He was far too foxed to continue any discussion. But when they exited the library, they left behind a gentleman whose conscience was beginning to smart.

Had he been wrong about Miss O'Donnell being an adventuress? Colin didn't know. What he knew was that she was an eccentric which could be just as damning in the eyes of Society, and she was Irish—

another black mark against her. Why, he would be improving her circumstance both socially and financially if he were to wed her.

He put down his glass of brandy and made his way up to his room. All the while, he wondered why his arguments seemed to ring hollow in his ears. It wasn't as if he had much choice in the matter. The next day was the seventh of June, and he had scarcely a week before he must wed. Miss O'Donnell would do as nicely as any other female, and she was at hand.

With that unhappy thought, Colin went to bed, determined to start wooing the Irish beauty on the following morning. Montmoorland was worth any sacrifice. But as the vision of Miss O'Donnell floated up his mind, he wondered if marriage to such a lady would be a sacrifice.

CHAPTER THREE

A rainstorm passed over Montmoorland during the night. By morning, the air was cool and the landscape glistened with droplets of water clinging to the leaves and grass as the bright sun rose in a cloudless sky. Colin stood at the window of his bedchamber, gazing at the land he loved. He knew every inch of the estate, every pasture, hill, and stream, but he'd come to a decision during the night that might well cost him his home.

He'd clearly taken leave of his senses when he decided to invite Miss O'Donnell and her uncle to the estate. It had been cruel and selfish to involve someone else—especially a young female like Moira—in his scheme to get revenge on his grand-mother. As the hours had ticked away the previous night and sleep escaped him, he remembered all she'd told them of her own situation in Ireland. The eldest of three sisters, she'd been the one to take over after her father's death had left her mother devastated. The young lady might have been unconventional, but she was no adventuress.

In truth, he'd come to realize that, much like himself, she was simply fighting in the best way she could to preserve her family estate. Fate had given her Eire's Luck. And while Colin had recklessly thought Moira was the solution to his problem, he'd finally come to the realization that he couldn't use her in such a despicable manner for his own gain.

Just then, movement in the rear pasture caught his eye. A horse and rider flashed across the open field with lightning speed. Colin knew at once he was watching the groom exercise the Irish stallion—a stallion he owned one-third share of.

He watched as the animal hurtled along the length of the stone fence, the rider hunched low on the steed's back, always asking for more speed. The horse galloped in a wide arch and continued his breakneck pace back toward the stables.

Colin's heart began to pound. Was it possible his share of that animal might be the solution to his financial problems? It was a well-known fact that the Irishman O'Kelly had become rich by putting the famous Eclipse to stud some fifty years earlier, after retiring the animal undefeated. Was there a chance that Eire's Luck could do the same for them?

In truth, Colin had paid little attention to the horse earlier, Miss O'Donnell being the object of his pursuit. Could he make a fortune with Eire's Luck and tell his grandmother to be damned? The young groom had ridden that horse with an amazing ability, and the animal seemed faster than anything Colin had ever witnessed.

But he was no greenling. He needed to go down and inspect the animal, possibly even match the horse against one of his own well-bred animals. He would go talk with Jim, Miss O'Donnell's groom and rider. The boy, no doubt, could tell him a great deal.

Colin dressed and left his room. He encountered Mr. Rourke in the upper hall and was amazed at the gentleman's bright-eyed appearance, considering the amount of whiskey he'd consumed the previous evening. "Good morning, sir. I'm surprised to see you up so early."

"To be sure, you were thinking I would still be totty this morning, but an Irishman can hold his drink, my lord." The two men fell into step and started down the Grand Staircase.

Colin smiled at the gentleman's resilience. "Do you wish to go down to the stables with me and watch Jim exercise Eire's Luck?"

Sean Rourke halted near the top of the stairs as Colin continued to descend. "No need to be bothering the groom. He's a fine lad and knows how to handle Lucky."

"I have no doubt the lad is able, but I just want to take a closer look at my investment—"

Colin's comment was cut off in midsentence as Mr. Rourke's body came hurling past him like a tree felled on a mountainside. The Irishman rolled down the wide, carpeted staircase, gaining speed until he landed on the black-and-white marble below. The gentleman groaned as he lay on the floor.

Colin dashed down the stairs and knelt beside his guest. "Mr. Rourke, are you injured?"

The Irishman groaned again, but did not open his eyes. Lord Lamont shouted for a servant, but since none were nearby in the understaffed manor, he rose and hurried to find someone to send for the doctor.

Sean Rourke lifted his head and opened one eye to make certain his lordship was gone; then he rubbed his aching shoulder. " 'Tis sure I am I'll earn every penny of my share of that horse before we leave this cursed land."

At the sound of Lord Lamont returning, the Irishman put his head back on the floor and again played his role to the hilt.

"I'm late, Doreen. We must hurry." Moira pulled the top of her simple green muslin gown over her shoulders; then the maid quickly tied her up behind.

"There's no rush, miss. The dinin' room was empty when I come past but minutes ago. Don't be expectin' two fashionable gentlemen like Lord Lamont and his friend to be risin' afore noon."

Moira hoped the girl was right. It would certainly make life simpler for them during their stay at Montmoorland. When the servant was finished doing up the gown, Moira took a seat at the small dressing table. She watched as the girl pulled her reddish-blond curls up into a Grecian knot atop her head, allowing ringlets to hang down. "It's Uncle Sean I worry about. You know how he is. If there is trouble to be had, he'll find it and gladly bring us along for the ride.''

The maid worked busily for a few minutes, then stepped back to admire her handy work. "Sure, and you're ready in under ten minutes.''

A knock sounded at the door startling both women. Moira called for the visitor to enter. The door opened to reveal Lord Lamont, a worried expression on his face.

"Miss O'Donnell, I apologize for disturbing you so early, but there has been a slight accident involving Mr. Rourke. I thought you might help convince him to allow me to summon the local physician.''

Moira rose and hurried to stand beside his lordship. The gentleman did disturb her, but not in the way he meant. She was amazed at how small and vulnerable she felt beside him. It was not a sensation she was used to, since she was rather self-sufficient. Then with a mental shake, she forced her mind to her uncle. "How was he injured, my lord?''

His lordship frowned. '' 'Tis a puzzle to me, but we were coming down for breakfast, and the next thing I knew the gentleman was rolling down the stairs. He doesn't appear to have broken any bones, but still I would feel better if Dr. Kent were to see him.''

"Take me to him, sir. I shall do my best to convince him, but he is as stubborn as your Mr. Higgins.''

The baron led Moira down to a small drawing room on the ground floor, where she found her uncle reclining on a worn chaise. There was no visible sign of injury, but Moira knew that meant little when dealing with a fall. She went to his side and placed a gentle hand on his shoulder.

"Uncle Sean, are you hurt?"

The Irishman opened one hazel-hued eye and quickly scanned the room. Spying his lordship, he slowly opened the other and gave his niece a piercing stare. "I'm in one piece as I assured Lord Lamont. You know how I hate having a fuss made when I have one of my spells."

Moira looked at him, puzzled. What spells did he mean? Then she realized she must take Uncle Sean's lead as he kept wiggling his eyebrows in a very odd manner. "Ah, you had a spell." She glanced at his lordship and forced a nervous smile. "I think there is nothing to worry about, sir. Just leave him in my capable hands, and he shall be fine after a bit of rest."

The baron looked doubtful. "Are you certain?"

"Oh, quite positive. Please don't let us detain you. I shall stay with him until he is more the thing."

"Shall I have Mrs. Jones bring you something to eat while you attend him?"

Moira's smile softened to a natural gesture at the gentleman's kindness. "That would be most welcome, my lord."

Lord Lamont left the drawing room. Moira turned to stare at her uncle, who grinned at her, but only put his finger over his lips in a gesture of silence. Within minutes, the housekeeper entered with a tray. The woman informed them they only had to use the bell and she would see to their further needs.

Moira glared at her uncle, who'd sat up the instant the drawing room door closed behind Mrs. Jones. He snatched up a piece of toast while he poured out two cups of coffee.

"Now, what is all this business about tumbling down stairs and having spells, Uncle?" She crossed her arms and waited for an explanation, but the gentleman's mouth was quite full.

At last, he brushed the toast crumbs from his fingers, then said, "I almost had a genuine spell when Lord Lamont informed me he was going to watch Eire's Luck exercise."

Moira's face turned pale and she slowly unfolded her arms, allowing them to drop to her side as she sat down on the nearest chair. "Why would he do that?"

"Wants to take a closer look at his investment, my dear."

"Did you tell him there was no need?"

"I tried but there was no talking the lad out of going, so there was nothing for it but to take a tumble." The Irishman rubbed his shoulder before adding, "It worked, but I can't be careening down a flight of stairs every morning to keep him away from Lucky."

Moira slumped back into the chair, staring at her uncle with defeat. She hadn't planned on Lord Lamont being involved in their plans, and she very much disliked being untruthful with him after his kindness to them. "Perhaps we should tell him the truth about Eire's Luck."

The Irishman shook his head. "Don't risk it, my

dear. We've too much riding on this to let some prim and proper Englishman put a period to our plans. If he's anything like the fashionable fribbles always coming to Cork to buy bloodstock, he'll soon find something new to draw his attention elsewhere. In the meantime, lass, I'm certain we can come up with a plan to keep the gentleman away from the stables in the morning."

"Like what?" Moira's blue eyes filled with hope.

"I guess I could fall out my window while admiring the sunrise tomorrow."

Moira stared at her uncle for a moment before she laughed at the absurdity of the suggestion. "The pair of us are more likely to end up in Newgate Prison instead of the winner's circle in York."

Sean smiled and handed his niece the cup of coffee he'd poured earlier. "You are forgetting about one thing."

"What is that?" Moira took the cup.

"Why, the luck of the Irish, lass. We'll come through this fine."

Moira hoped there was such a thing as true luck. They would need every bit they could get in York for all to go right on race day.

Colin did not see Miss O'Donnell or Mr. Rourke again until that evening. The Irishman told amusing tales at the table and appeared in the best of spirits, but the young lady seemed a bit subdued as she listened to her uncle spin his yarns. Colin attributed it to her concern for the older gentleman's health, but in the baron's mind, there seemed to be nothing wrong with the fellow, except a fondness for drink.

When the covers were removed and Miss O'Donnell rose to leave, Colin was surprised that her uncle offered to keep her company in the drawing room. As the pair departed, Nigel came to sit near Colin as Larkin poured two brandies.

"How was your trip into York?" the baron asked his friend even as his gaze lingered on the door through which his guests had departed. He was curious about what was bothering Moira.

Nigel took a sip of his brandy before saying, " 'Twas vastly entertaining. You should have joined me. The town is filling up with race enthusiasts come for the big day. Saw some excellent steeds being touted as the next winner. Our bragging Irish friend is likely to have the wind taken out of his sails when he sees the competition." Seeing his companion was barely paying any heed to him, Nigel sighed, then asked, "So how goes your plan to marry the lovely Miss O'Donnell?"

Colin shook his head. "I shan't. You were right last night. It would be very wrong of me to use the lady simply to get back at my grandmother. I've decided that, with my share of the winnings from Eire's Luck, I'll be able to tell Grandmama she might do as she pleases with her fortune."

His glass of brandy nearly to his lips, Nigel paused and stared at his friend. He'd watched the way Colin's eyes had followed Miss O'Donnell from the time she'd entered the dining room until she'd departed. The baron might think he'd given up his plan, but clearly he was drawn to the lady.

While Lady Ferries might forgive her grandson's refusal to wed at her command, Nigel suspected, from what Colin had said, that the dowager would never pardon him for marrying an Irishwoman. The baron seemed besotted, for he was speaking as if Eire's Luck were destined to win. Abruptly, Nigel put down his glass and rose. He had to protect his friend from himself, and the only way he knew to do so was to capture the lady's attentions. "Shall we remove to the drawing room?"

Colin agreed, wondering at Nigel's sudden desire to be in company with Sean Rourke. They joined the others in the Rose Drawing Room on the ground floor. Miss O'Donnell and her uncle stood beside a chessboard. As the lady examined the intricately carve pieces, Mr. Rourke spoke intently to her.

At the entry of the gentlemen, the Irishman fell silent and the lady accidently toppled several of the chess pieces when she hurriedly tried to put the knight back into position.

"Oh, my lord, I do apologize. I was just admiring the unusual style of the chessmen."

Colin came to stand beside the lady, smiling down at her as she straightened all the wooden chessmen. "They are Spanish in design. An old friend, knowing my fondness for chess, sent them to me from the Peninsula when he was with Wellington's army."

"Now there is an Irishman who did us proud," Sean said pointedly to Nigel.

Nigel smiled benignly. "My father said there is always an exception to every rule."

As the two men glared at one another, Colin hurriedly asked, "Do you play, Miss O'Donnell?"

"I am but a tolerable player, sir. If you would like a good game, my uncle is the opponent you wish."

Colin had no wish to be sitting across a chessboard from Sean Rourke. He'd only offered the question to distract the two men from their verbal sparring, but before he could say a word, Nigel stepped to the lady and offered her his arm.

"An excellent notion, dear lady. Colin might indulge in one of his favorite pastimes of annihilating another player and I shall take you to the terrace, where it is quite fine this evening." Without waiting for anyone to agree, Nigel swept Miss O'Donnell through the double glass doors that opened on the garden.

Sean Rourke took a seat in front of the board. "Since I am visiting, I shall be white." He then advanced his rook and looked at Colin expectantly.

Manners demanded that Colin play his guest, so he took his seat and made a move. But no sooner was the piece in position than his gaze returned to the pair strolling up and down the terrace. As the sound of Miss O'Donnell's laughter floated into the drawing room on the warm night air, Colin found himself wishing to trade places with his friend.

The baron was so distracted watching the couple outside that Mr. Rourke had captured a great many of his chessmen by the time Miss O'Donnell again entered the drawing room to announce she was retiring.

When Nigel placed a lingering kiss on the lady's hand before she departed, Colin suddenly was over-whelmed with the urge to plant his friend a facer. Then he wondered what had come over himself. Had he not decided that the lady was not for him?

At last, the two chess players were left alone with their game, but Colin's distraction had left him with too few pieces to properly defend himself and within some ten minutes the game was ended, Mr. Rourke the winner.

"Good game, my lord, but I think you were not playing your best. Perhaps in the morning your thoughts will be clearer and you will be more up to the challenge."

"In the morning? I have things I must attend in the morning. I cannot play again until after nuncheon. Besides, I wish to be present to closely observe Eire's Luck during his exercise. Does Miss O'Donnell usually watch the horse's training sessions?" Colin was hoping to get a chance to see the lady without Nigel hanging on her sleeve as he'd done tonight.

"Moira? Never, sir. She trusts Jim to work Lucky properly. Her father, Sir Curran, trained the lad him-self, so there is nothing to worry about. Now, sir, if you'll excuse me, I want to speak with Moira before she falls asleep."

Disappointed he wouldn't be seeing Moira at the stables, Colin made no comment except to wish the Irishman good night as he rose to leave. Left alone in the drawing room, Colin wondered at his desire to see the lady alone.

Was he falling in love? The notion was too absurd. She was beautiful and enticing—that was all. He desired her, but nothing more. Trying to push the thoughts of Miss O'Donnell from his mind, he rose and made his way upstairs.

On the upper landing, he paused when he heard a shuffling sound. He gazed down the dark hallway toward the west wing, but could see nothing. Worrying his decaying home might have become infested with rats, he turned and morosely made his way to his chamber in the east wing.

The night before, his conscience had kept him awake, but fatigue helped him put his worries aside. He quickly fell asleep, only to be disturbed by dreams of the Irish beauty. He awoke the following morning thinking perhaps it was best that the lady wouldn't be at the stables. She was too enticing for her own good, and it would be some time before Eire's Luck could generate enough income to see Colin out of his financial straits. With a promise to concentrate on the horse and not the lady, he dressed.

He went to the door and turned the handle, but nothing happened. Thinking the door was merely stuck, he again turned the handle and tugged with a great deal of force. Once more, nothing happened. His gaze dropped to the lock, and he noticed for the first time that the key was missing.

Damnation, someone had locked him in his room.

CHAPTER FOUR

Montmoorland's vast size and greatly reduced staff conspired to leave Lord Lamont stranded in his room until almost noon that day. At first, he yanked the bellpull to summon a servant; then he remembered the rope had broken some months earlier and he'd neglected to have it repaired. With determination, he went back to the door and hammered on the oaken portal while shouting for Mrs. Jones. But after some thirty minutes with no response, he gave up in a considerable rage, his knuckles aching from the abuse.

The window of his bedchamber proved little help as well. Colin waved a handkerchief and shouted as the only gardener still employed trimmed a tree some distance from the manor, but his lordship's efforts were to no avail. The old man was near seventy and deaf as the stone lions perched on the pillars at the entry gates.

In frustration, Colin slumped into a chair and put his mind to the questions of who had locked the door and why. His thoughts went at once to the two strangers residing at Montmoorland, but what reason could Miss O'Donnell or her peculiar uncle have to want to keep him a prisoner? Perhaps the race, but that was not to take place for another week. There didn't seem to be anything he could think of that would make them engage in such a prank.

Then the memory of his conversation with Nigel in the library two nights earlier returned. Had his friend not threatened to lock Colin in until he'd come to his senses? But Colin had changed his mind. He'd told Nigel that using Miss O'Donnell was no longer a part of his plan. So why would Nigel resort to such a foolhardy trick?

By the time the small ormolu clock on the mantelpiece chimed the hour of twelve, Colin was famished. In frustration, he once again marched to the door and began to pound on the wood with his closed fist.

Within minutes, he heard someone call his name through the thick wood. "Who's there?" Colin shouted.

" 'Tis I, Nigel. What the devil are you about to be making such a racket?"

"Unlock this door!"

There was a slight delay; then a click sounded and the door opened. His anger in control of him, Colin barreled through the portal and grabbed his startled friend by the lapels. His momentum took both men all the way across the hall, where Nigel's head banged the opposite wall with a resounding thump.

"What do you mean locking me in my room?" Colin demanded.

Nigel Anson stared at his friend with a hint of fear as he rubbed his head. "Are you all about in the head? I was coming down the hall going to the breakfast parlor. I heard your hammering and came to see what was amiss. Why the blazes would I lock you in your room? Value my chin too much to risk one of your facers."

Colin could see no guile in his friend's face. Slowly, he released his hold on Nigel's coat. "Then who would have locked me in?"

Smoothing out the crumpled kerseymere lapels, Nigel speculated, "If I were to hazard a guess, I'd put my money on that rogue Rourke. Ought to go down and see if you still have any silver left in the house."

"Well, I don't need to because my father cleaned the manor out years ago of anything of value save the little bit that we dined with last evening." But Colin's thought settled on Sean Rourke as the best suspect. Why would the Irishman wish to lock Colin in his room?

Nigel, edging round his lordship, said, "If you've decided I'm not the culprit, might I at least go and have my breakfast after being so grossly abused, old fellow? I must say it puzzles me why you think I was the one."

Colin fell into step with his friend, and they made

their way toward the breakfast parlor. "Because you said you would do that very thing the other night."

"Did I? Must have been dreadfully foxed, for I haven't the least memory of babbling such foolishness."

Hunger stayed Colin's need to confront anyone about the locked door. The gentlemen were able to have breakfast in peace, Miss O'Donnell and Mr. Rourke being nowhere about. But no sooner had Colin finished than he set out to find Moira. He was certain he could get honest answers from her.

He soon found the lady in the library, searching for a book to entertain herself with. She smiled at him as he entered, and he was struck with the sudden urge to take her in his arms and kiss that delectable mouth. Deciding he'd been too long without a mistress, he pushed the thought from his mind and concentrated on finding out the truth.

After a few moments of polite greetings, he got straight to the point. "Miss O'Donnell, I apologize for disturbing you but I think your uncle locked me in my room last night."

Delicate brows rose in surprise at his stark announcement. There was a look of shock on the young lady's beautiful face, but Colin would swear there was no surprise.

Her gaze dropped to the book in her hand, and she bit nervously on her full lower lip as if she didn't know what to say.

At last, guilty blue eyes looked at him. "My lord, I was afraid of something like this."

"You knew he might lock me in my room?" Colin's body stiffened in shock. Was the lady involved?

"Not exactly. I had no notion what he intended, I do assure you. 'Tis only that he come to my room last night and swore that . . . Well, sir, he swore that you had designs on my virtue." The lady turned and walked away from Colin even as she continued. "Uncle Sean was afraid . . . you intended to come to my chambers."

Colin was glad she had her back to him, or she would have seen guilt written all over his face. He had watched her like some moonstruck pup the previous night. Her uncle might appear the fool, but the wily old fox had detected Colin's growing desire for Moira. Yet surely the Irishman must have realized that Colin would never step over the line of what was proper with a genteel lady. Marriage was for women like Moira, and Colin suspected she would only take such a step for love. Schooling his features, he moved to where she stood, looking out the windows.

"Miss O'Donnell, I cannot deny that I greatly admire your beauty. But let me assure you that I would never make improper advances on a delicately bred female staying in my home."

The Irish beauty gave him an embarrassed smile, a stain of scarlet coloring her cheeks. "Sir, I believe you an honorable gentleman and so I told my uncle. I can only apologize for his conduct and say that, if you should like, we shall leave Montmoorland this very day."

Suddenly their gazes locked and their breathing came in unison. Colin was filled with an overwhelming need to possess the woman. She stood staring back at him with an innocence that teased at his soul.

The sound of a harness jingling in front of the manor penetrated the stillness in the library, breaking the spell of intimacy. Colin came to his senses and realized he hadn't responded to her announcement. "I have no wish for you to leave my home. You and Mr. Rourke are welcome for as long as you wish. I would merely request that you convince your uncle I am not in the habit of forcing unwanted attentions on ladies."

The noise of the front knocker being pounded repeatedly echoed through the house. Colin excused himself, saying he must go see who had arrived, for his butler had gone in to York that morning on business.

Moira stood beside the window, her thoughts in turmoil after the gentleman departed. *Were* Lord Lamont's attentions unwanted? She knew that he stirred something deep in her that she'd never before felt—something mysterious and exciting, yet dangerous for all her plans.

Then her thoughts turned to her capricious relative. Good heavens, her uncle had actually locked his lordship in his room to keep him away from Eire's Luck. With a determined sigh, she decided she needed to speak with Uncle Sean at once.

She exited the library through a door that was designed to look like the other windows. Then she made her way toward the stables. Scarcely halfway there, she encountered the Irishman, whistling as he made his way back to the manor.

Moira halted and waited until the gentleman

strolled up to her. "Uncle Sean, I shall lock you in *your* room if you pull another outlandish trick on Lord Lamont."

Without the least remorse, the gentleman grinned. "It accomplished what I wanted, did it not? Is his lordship in a dreadful taking?"

"He was, but I fobbed him off with a ridiculous story about you thinking he had designs on me and was planning some midnight tryst. He seemed to accept the Banbury tale I spun, but you cannot keep doing such strange things or he will have us both committed to an asylum for the insane."

Sean wasn't so certain the tale his niece had spun was so ridiculous, having seen the way his lordship's gaze followed Moira. It was a pity Lord Lamont's finances seemed to be as dire as their own, or Sean might have encouraged the girl to cast out lures to the baron. But as matters stood there was no point.

"Take a look around you, lass. The gentleman has a need for what Eire's Luck can provide. He might fret and fume about these odd occurrences, but he's not likely to be showing us the door."

Moira nodded as her gaze swept the unkempt expanse of lawn. If all went as planned, she would be providing Lord Lamont with the means to bring Montmoorland back to its former glory. Still, her conscience bothered her at the subterfuge. "I just wish we could be honest with his lordship."

"We're not being dishonest, Moira. We simply haven't told the laddie all there is to know about the horse. We cannot risk losing this opportunity over such a trifling matter. Think of your mother and your sisters, lass. They are depending on us.''

Uncle Sean was right. She had no business letting down her guard and endangering all their plans. She had her family to think about. Yet a pair of smiling amber eyes kept coming to her doubt-filled mind.

''Come, my dear. Let us defy propriety and sneak round to the kitchens to see what the friendly Mrs. Jones might offer up to two starving people who rose far too early. 'Tis hunger that nags at you and nothing more.''

Moira allowed herself to be drawn to the rear of the manor. After all, their little deception wouldn't hurt anyone and they would each benefit. With that thought, she had to be content.

Harry Banks brushed road dust from his ten-tier gray driving cape as he watched his groom lead the hired curricle and team toward the stables. He wasn't happy about being forced to drive all the way from London at a breakneck pace, but his mother would have settled for nothing less.

All the fuss and urgency had begun with a scrawled letter his grandmother had sent from Fernbrook, where she'd gone to visit her sister. The missive contained an amazing tale about Lady Ferries's intention of cutting off his cousin, Colin, without so much as a farthing unless he was wed by the fifteenth of June. His grandmother had hinted that with a little initiative on Harry's part, he might never need worry about funds again. She would do her part to praise Harry to Lady Ferries, but he would have to keep a close watch on Colin and, if possible, keep the baron from marrying.

Mrs. Banks, upon receipt of the letter, had embraced the plan wholeheartedly and summoned her son. The lady followed the Society news closely and was well aware that Lord Lamont had never been linked to a female to whom he could offer his hand. And so there Harry was at Montmoorland, to see if Lamont was actively pursuing a bride.

For Harry's part, he thought it all a hum. Even if the dowager did issue such a command, Colin would have gone to London to look for a proper female. He would not have come home to the remote tumbled-down manor. As Harry's gaze scanned the crumbling facade, the door opened to reveal his cousin.

With a practiced flourish, the young dandy tossed one side of his driving cape back over his shoulder to reveal a primrose yellow superfine coat over fawn buckskins. "Good afternoon, Lamont."

"Harry! What the devil are you doing in Yorkshire?" Lord Lamont barked, distractedly. It was not that he disliked Harry, even with his outlandish clothes. In truth, he hardly knew the silly fellow, which made his visit all the more surprising. It was only that the young man appeared something of a fribble, having no estate to inherit, no profession, and no inclination to seek his fortune in any manner at all.

"I was up in Carlisle rusticating. Decided to return to London and knew you wouldn't mind if I broke my journey here for a few days." The falsehood his mother had concocted flowed from Harry's lips with ease. He was not a deep young man; left to his own devices, he would never have thought to come to Yorkshire to see what the baron was doing in regard to finding a bride. But Mrs. Banks possessed all the ambition her son lacked and had sent him on his way full of instructions.

"You are welcome at Montmoorland anytime, Cousin. I fear, however, that I cannot offer you much in the way of entertainment, and I have reduced the staff so greatly that all your needs may not be met as quickly as you might wish." Colin was full of doubt about the reason for Harry's presence. Clearly something drastic must have occurred to drive him from Town, but the baron's mind was too full of Moira O'Donnell and her suggestion that she leave the manor to be concerned with his cousin's affairs.

Harry waved his hand dismissively. "Oh, I'm never the least trouble to have about. You shan't even notice I am here. I insist that you go do whatever you were doing before I arrived. I am capable of amusing myself tolerably well, Cousin."

Colin, hoping to return to the library and again see Moira, was perfectly content to do as his guest advised. He yanked the bellpull for Mrs. Jones. When that lady arrived, he told her to take Harry upstairs to a room and to see that he had some refreshments to tide him over until dinner that evening. He warned his cousin that they kept country hours and would dine at seven.

As the pair disappeared up the Grand Staircase, Colin hurried back to the library, but was disappointed to find the room empty. He hoped Moira wouldn't feel it necessary that she and her demented uncle leave Montmoorland. As he stared out the window, he knew it was not just Eire's Luck that made him want her to stay. Moira had touched something deep within him.

A sense of defeat burned in Harry Banks's chest as he stared across the table at the young lady who'd been introduced as Miss O'Donnell. All he could do was lament the stroke of fate that had thrown the chit into his cousin's path. His family's plans for securing a fortune were fading before his eyes. With a sigh, he picked up his glass and gulped down the entire contents, then signaled the butler to fill it again.

Across the table, Moira watched the London gentleman with curiosity. His reaction when she and Uncle Sean had entered the drawing room that evening had been strange to say the least. He'd forgotten himself to such an extent that he'd demanded, "Who the blazes is that?"

Lord Lamont had made the introductions, explaining about his guests and Eire's Luck, but the young man had stared at Moira as if she'd come down dressed only in her petticoat. Clearly, she disturbed him in some unfathomable way, for he'd begun to mutter strangely to himself. But when his lordship had inquired if there was a problem, Mr. Banks had denied any distress and fallen silent, continuing to stare at her with a sullen slant to his thin lips.

The dandy sat ignoring the people around him, pushing the food on his plate about with distraction.

Suddenly, his gaze riveted on Moira and he interrupted the conversation. "O''Donnell. That's Irish,
isn't it?"

Surprised at the gentleman's strange tone, Moira
said, "It is, sir."

Harry smiled at her for the first time that evening;
then he began to eat his meal with relish, offering
no other comment. He'd suddenly remembered that
Lady Ferries disliked the Irish with a passion. Why,
all he needed to do was return to Fernbrook and
announce that his cousin had taken it into his head
to marry an Irishwoman, and everything would go as
he and his mother had planned. He would leave first
thing in the morning.

A strange silence followed Harry's abrupt question,
and Lord Lamont covered the awkwardness with an
invitation to Moira to walk in the garden after they'd
dined, the weather being particularly fine that evening. The prospect was so enticing, it pushed all
thoughts of the odd Mr. Banks from Moira's mind.

When the moment finally arrived and his lordship
offered Moira his arm, her fingers tingled at the feel
of the black fabric of his evening coat beneath her
fingers. As he led her into the fading darkness, she
looked up to see him eyeing her intently.

"I am glad of this opportunity to have a few
moments' private conversation with you. It is my hope
that you stay at Montmoorland until after the races,
Miss O'Donnell."

Moira wondered if they would still be welcome by
then if her uncle continued his pranks. "We shall,

sir, as long as you can tolerate my uncle's strange turns."

Lord Lamont laughed, glancing briefly over his shoulder at the men clearly visible in the drawing room. Sean Rourke and Nigel Anson could be seen arguing the merits of a painting over the fireplace, while Mr. Banks peered into the near darkness at them. "We all have our peculiar relations. But tell me, what are your plans if Eire's Luck becomes a sensation and leaves you an heiress? Shall it be a Season in London for you? Or will you return to Ireland to your mother and sisters?"

Moira sighed at the comforting thought of returning home and leaving all this business behind. There was a sadness to her tone when she said, "My lord, it shall be quite some time before I am able to see my family or my home. Uncle Sean says that to make Eire's Luck a truly valuable sire we must spend the better part of this next year going from race to race."

Colin detected a hint of homesickness in the lady's tone. A thought occurred to him that he might make it possible for her to return home at once, yet even as the idea came to him, he realized he didn't want Moira to go. Still, he didn't like the notion that she was unhappy.

"I could handle all the details of racing Eire's Luck and keep watch on Mr. Rourke if you should like to leave matters in our hands and return to Ireland after the races at York."

Moira's gaze flew to his, a hint of tears welling up in their blue depths. "You are . . . too kind, my lord.

We don't deserve such kindness considering . . . What I mean is, I could never leave Lucky alone. Please excuse me, but I feel the headache coming on. I shall retire early."

Without waiting for him to accompany her, the young lady turned and hurried back toward the manor, disappearing through the drawing room door. He stood bemused, wondering what had upset Moira so. Did she not trust him to be honest about the animal's winnings? Or did she think him unable to keep her uncle in check? Colin found he was left with more questions than answers and decided that women were too often a puzzle.

Not wishing to spend an evening making small talk with Harry or listening to Mr. Rourke and Nigel argue everything under the sun, Colin turned and walked to the stables. After all, he still hadn't gotten a chance to take a close look at the stallion that might change his future.

The stable was lit by a single lantern hanging from a beam in the middle. As Colin passed his own horses, he stroked the nose of one of the grays, which had come to the stall door at the sound of footsteps approaching. As he drew near Eire's Luck, the chestnut began to pace restlessly in his stall. The closer Colin got, the more agitated the animal became. By the time he stood at the door of the stall, the animal had begun to whinny and dance at the rear of the small enclosure.

Just then, Miss O'Donnell's groom stepped out of the tack room. "Oh, 'tis you, my lord. Would there be somethin' you'd be needin'?"

"Jim, you are just the person I wanted to see. I have a few questions about Lucky here."

The red-haired Irish lad looked doubtful, but came up to where his lordship stood. He spoke to the horse in a soothing voice; at once the animal calmed down, but it remained in the back of the stall. "Sure, and what would you be wantin' to know, sir?"

Colin watched the animal thoughtfully. "He seems a bit too high-strung, Jim. If he gets this frightened by a stranger at his stall, however does he manage with a field of strange horses?"

The groom looked down at his muck-covered boots, seeming to think about what to say. At last, he gazed at the horse and said, "Well, to be sure the prad's a highbred 'un, but with a rider on his back, he's as docile as a lamb. Don't need to be worryin' bout him not bein' able to race. Left 'em speechless at Cork, he did, when he run off and left the lot of them gallopers."

Despite Jim's reassurances, Colin still harbored doubts. "I think I shall come down and race one of my horses against him in the morning. See how he does with a little competition."

The lad frowned. "I reckon you aught to be speakin' with Miss Moira or Mr. Sean about doin' somethin' like that, my lord. Sure I am it ain't my place to be sayin' how things is managed."

"And so I shall, Jim." Colin decided he would go at once and speak with Rourke about arranging a mock race for the morning. Colin was certain he would feel more comfortable knowing that the high-strung Lucky wasn't likely to shy or bolt on race day.

He bid the groom good night and returned to the manor.

Upon entering the drawing room, Colin discovered that Nigel and Mr. Rourke had ceased hostilities long enough to play a game of piquet. His cousin had already retired for the night, which was surprising behavior for one used to the late nights in London.

At last, the gentlemen ended their game, and Colin was able to draw the Irishman aside to announce his intention to race against Eire's Luck.

A shadow seemed to settle in the older gentleman's hazel eyes, and he shook his head. "Don't be going down and disturbing Lucky's practice runs, my lord. Moira don't like people inferring with that horse when he's preparing for a race."

Colin looked down his nose at Mr. Rourke. "I have no intention of disturbing the horse, sir. I don't think I need remind you I own a share of the animal and have every right to participate in his training."

"But there's no—"

"I intend to go in the morning, sir," Colin stated with finality. "I shall bid you all good night."

As he made his way up the stairs, Colin was struck by the fact that Sean Rourke had been determined from the first day that he not visit the stables while the stallion was training. Was there something wrong with the horse?

Then his thoughts returned to Moira and her distress in the garden earlier in the evening. Was that why she had been so upset? Was there something amiss with her prized horse about which she was afraid to tell him?

Colin didn't have a clue what was going on, but he was determined to be at the stables early the next day. After that, he would find Miss Moira O'Donnell and have a conversation with her about Eire's Luck.

CHAPTER FIVE

Colin rose early, determined to make it to the stables before the groom exercised Eire's Luck. To his surprise, he arrived in the front hall to find his cousin preparing to depart. Harry seemed in a great hurry, so Colin didn't linger over their good-byes. He distractedly bid the gentleman farewell, his mind full of the mystery of the Irish horse.

As the carriage rolled away, Colin said to his butler, "I shall be at the st—"

The baron froze as his gaze caught sight of smoke drifting from under the door of the Yellow Salon. He dashed to the double doors and thrust them open. Thick gray smoke boiled into the front hall. Without regard for his safety, Colin fanned his way through the choking cloud to the two sets of glass doors on the opposite side of the room. He threw open each door, and within minutes, the room began to clear.

Larkin, having entered the room, stood by the fireplace. "Here's the trouble, my lord. Some scoundrel's lit a fire of dirty rags with the flue closed." The old butler used a poker to force the hot handle inside the chimney open even as he coughed and choked on the fumes.

Colin surveyed the chamber through the thinning smoke. He suspected there had been no real danger or damage to the room that a little airing wouldn't fix, but he realized at once that he'd been subjected to another incident to keep him away from the stables. Well, it wouldn't work that morning.

"Larkin, have you seen Mr. Rourke this morning?"

"He breakfasted early, sir, but I can't say where the gentleman is at the moment."

Probably far away from the Yellow Salon so no one would accuse him of starting the fire. Colin kept his suspicions to himself, merely saying, "Inform Mrs. Jones of this mishap, and tell her to make certain this room is aired properly. I have urgent business elsewhere."

The baron crossed the terrace and hurried through the gardens to the stables. As he entered the building, he could see Lucky's stall stood empty. He strode down the aisle and out the rear doors.

The animal was at a full gallop on the back side of the pasture. Moira's groom was urging Lucky onward, but the boy was hunched so low on the horse's back that Colin could only see the top of his hat. Lucky thundered toward the stables with grace, determination, and stunning speed.

Colin, feeling foolish for having doubts about the animal's abilities, felt his heart plummet when suddenly the groom's hat flew up in the air, exposing Moira's reddish-blond curls. A feeling of foreboding began to fill the young lord. He clung to the slender hope that the lady was just doing the groom's job due to his being ill; then Colin remembered that Jim had been hale and hearty the previous evening. Surely she didn't think she was going to ride the horse in York?

The moment Moira's gaze settled on his lordship, a flush warmed her cheeks. Keeping her distance, she slowed the horse to a walk and began to make large circles in the pasture to allow the animal to cool. She could tell by the rigid look on Lord Lamont's face that he was angry, and she was frightened to tell him the truth.

At last, knowing she could no longer delay the confrontation, she put Lucky into a slow trot toward the stable and called for Jim. The lad appeared from inside the building. He tugged his hat at Lord Lamont, but moved past the gentleman to take the horse's reins as Moira dismounted.

"Walk him for fifteen minutes before you stable him, Jim."

"Aye, miss." The groom led the horse back into the pasture at a slow, ambling gait as Moira gazed at the advancing baron.

He stopped directly in front of her and crossed his arms over his chest. "Now, Miss O'Donnell, shall we have no more tricks and falsehoods about Eire's Luck? Why are you riding him instead of Jim?"

Moira bit her lip for a moment, then decided his lordship deserved the truth. "Because Lucky won't allow anyone on him but me."

The gentleman's amber eyes seemed to darken to mahogany. "And you intend to go to York dressed like a groom and ride on race day? To be gaped at by every gentleman and country farmer alike?"

Moira's back straightened at his angry tone. "I do, sir, but you needn't worry—"

"I forbid it!"

"How dare you! You have no right to forbid me anything. I shall race Lucky and I shall win and there is nothing you can do or say—"

Without warning his hands were on her arms and he drew her to him. "Do you have any idea how dangerous such a race will be, with all the bumping and jostling for position? And even were you lucky enough to win, do you think that no one will suspect you a female? You delude yourself, my dear."

Moira made a halfhearted attempt to pull away, but despite her anger at what he was saying, she liked the feel of his chest pressed against her. The sensations surging through her body made her struggle to put together her thoughts. "I can win. . . . I know I can."

His grip softened, and he lifted a hand up to trace the line of her jaw. "I suspect that you could, Moira. But they would never allow a woman to win a race. It would be a scandal. Besides, this is not some country contest. 'Tis one of the largest races in England. I couldn't bear it if you were hurt or killed."

With that, he lifted her chin and captured her mouth with his own. Moira was shocked at her own eager response to his lips. As a swirl of strange but wonderful new feelings surged through her, she realized she'd fallen in love with Lord Lamont.

At last, Colin lifted his head and gazed down into Moira's blue eyes, which stared back in wonder. He wasn't sure just when he'd known he loved her; he only knew that he couldn't live without her. "I love you, my darling Irish lass."

The lady's cheeks grew pink, but she said, "I love you, my lord."

"Then promise me you will give up this dangerous notion of racing Lucky at York." When the lady began to protest, Colin placed a finger over her lovely lips, quieting her. "I promise we shall race him later, after we find someone capable of riding him. A male someone."

Moira shook her head. "I don't think Lucky will allow—"

"He will if we give him time and find the right person. Now, enough about the horse. Say you will marry me."

The lady's eyes widened; then a smile settled on her lovely lips. "I will marry you, my dear love."

For the next fifteen minutes or more, the pair were scarcely aware of their surroundings as they surrendered to the sweetness of their feelings. At last, Colin drew reluctantly away from Moira and gave her a sheepish smile. "My dear, I have something to tell you and I hope you will agree."

The gentleman quickly explained about his grandmother's legacy and her edict about his being wed by the fifteenth of June. Would she object to being married by special license at the end of the week?

Moira tilted her head a bit as she gazed up at him. "I begin to think this marriage is the reason we were invited here and not Lucky."

Colin stroked a finger across her cheek. "I cannot deny there is some truth in what you say. But I knew from the first day you were at Montmoorland you were too much an innocent to be involved in my schemes. Then I fell in love with you, and I tell you now, even if my grandmother doesn't approve my choice, I will still be the winner."

Seeing the depth of feeling in the gentleman's amber eyes, Moira believed him. She would have liked to invite her mother and sisters to her wedding, but being a practical female, Moira realized it would be foolish to throw away a possible fortune. "What will a special license entail?"

Colin kissed her, then smiled. "I shall have to leave for London in the morning. In four days' time, I shall return and we can be married at the village church."

Moira gazed off in the distance. In four days' time was the race. She'd expected to be changing her circumstances on the back of her horse. Instead, she would be standing in front of a vicar. Glancing up at his lordship, her heart filled and she felt no regret. She loved him and was certain that, whatever happened with Lucky or his grandmother, she wouldn't regret her decision. "Then I will anxiously await your return."

Colin again captured Moira's mouth with his own.

The pair were so involved in the newness of their love they had no thoughts or worries about the future.

At last, they knew they must return to the manor and inform their friends and family of the news of their engagement and impending marriage. But only Nigel was to be found.

He said all that was proper, wishing Moira well, but it wasn't until the young lady left to change for dinner that he took Colin to task over his decision.

"She is a lovely lady, but you know your grandmother may not approve of Miss O'Donnell as your wife."

Colin shook his head. "I know, but I love her, Nigel. Grandmother may do with her money what she will. I intend to marry Moira on Friday."

Nigel, seeing the look in his friend's eyes, knew that Lamont was truly in love and would even risk a fortune for his Irish lady love. "So you will try to make Lady Ferries's deadline even though she might not be pleased with your choice. Do you want me to accompany you to London to get the license?"

"I should be delighted to have the company, but I warn you I depart before dawn in the morning."

Nigel groaned. "Now I realize why I have never been in love. It requires too much effort."

Colin laughed. "But 'tis worth it my friend. You will see so when your time comes."

Nigel hoped his time might never come if it meant he had to risk everything for the woman he loved, but he didn't voice his thoughts to Colin. Instead, the gentlemen settled on a time for their departure for London the following day.

* * *

The day was well advanced when Sean Rourke entered Montmoorland by way of the front door. He'd made himself scarce, knowing there would be a great to-do about the fire he'd set to keep Lord Lamont from the stables. While he hadn't remained to see the results of his grievous work, he'd been certain the trick would work without doing much harm.

He decided to retire to one of the small parlors in the rear of the house, hoping to delay the meeting with his lordship. He chose one referred to as the Velvet Parlor, then froze in the doorway when he discovered his niece and the baron standing before the fireplace, locked in a passionate embrace.

"What is the meaning of this, sir?" Sean roared.

The couple parted, but showed not the least embarrassment at being caught in such a compromising situation. Sean didn't like the looks they were giving him.

"So, at last you return, Rourke. Can I safely assume you have not burned down any building in my holdings?"

The Irishman was amazed that his lordship actually smiled when he asked the question. Certain it was a trick, Sean blustered, "Don't know what you mean, my lord. And kindly unhand my niece before I feel obliged to call you out."

Moira came toward him, her hands extended. "Oh, Uncle Sean, there is no need for any more tricks. Colin and I are to be married."

Shocked at the sudden turn of events, Sean took his niece's hands, but looked over her shoulder at his lordship. "Knows about Lucky, does he?"

Moira nodded her head, but it was Lord Lamont who spoke. "Forget about the horse for the moment. I leave for London in the morning to secure a special license. Moira and I will be married on Friday."

"After the race?" Sean was beginning to get a very bad feeling about the new situation.

"Forget about the race, Rourke. I won't allow my fiancée to be involved in such a venture."

"Forget about . . ." Sean grabbed his niece by the shoulders. "Moira, have you taken leave of your senses? This race was the reason we came to England. The pair of you fancy yourselves in love, but what about money to live on? You haven't two farthings to rub together between you."

His lordship came over and gently drew his fiancée away from the irate Irishman. "We fully intend to race Eire's Luck at a future date—after we find a man who can manage the animal. Don't look so forlorn. You will still be a wealthy man, simply at some later time."

Sean gazed from Moira to Lord Lamont, and he knew there would be no changing their minds. They were in love and foolish enough to think that all would be well. All his hopes were dashed. He had too much money wagered on the outcome of the York race to be delighted with his niece's marriage. With a sigh, he walked out of the Velvet Parlor without giving them his blessing. He was in no mood to celebrate a marriage that would put a period to all his plans.

The distraught Irishman wandered into the library, where he was soon drowning his sorrows in Irish whiskey. When Larkin arrived some thirty minutes later to announce dinner, Sean declared he wouldn't be joining the happy couple and Mr. Anson.

Fearful they would come looking for him, Sean poured himself another glassful of the potent amber liquid, then slipped out the side door unseen. He took his time making his way down to the stables, feeling sorry for himself and lamenting the twists of fate that had snatched away his good fortune just as he was about to grasp it in his hands. At last, he entered the stables. He made his way along the aisle of horses until he stood in front of Lucky. He gazed mournfully at the chestnut stallion on whom he'd penned his hopes.

Frustration seemed to well up in him, and he tossed the nearly empty glass against the rear door. "All is lost."

Jim's head poked out the tack room door at the sound of breaking glass. "Mr. Sean, sure and you're lookin' in a tweak."

When the gentleman turned toward the groom, he began to sway as if he might fall down. The lad hurried from the room and led the older man over to a stack of fresh hay, where he collapsed into a heap.

"Jim, the lass has gone and fallen in love with his lordship. Lucky ain't to race in York on Friday." Sean leaned back into the hay and snorted. "There's to be a wedding instead."

The groom looked surprised. "A weddin', sir. So soon?"

"Lamont's leaving in the morning for London for one of those special licenses. Wants the wedding when he returns on Friday."

Jim looked over at Eire's Luck, a thoughtful expression on his face. He remained quiet for some minutes while Sean Rourke vented his spleen about foolish females and love. When the gentleman fell silent, the groom said, "So his lordship's goin' to be gone for four days."

"Aye, it will take him that long to get to London and back." Sean was scarcely paying attention to Jim, his thoughts so full of his disappointment.

"Four days, sir. Sure I am that a great deal can happen in four days."

Sean sat up. "What are you thinking, lad?"

Jim leaned forward and laid out a plan to Sean Rourke, keeping his voice low, as if someone might overhear. The two argued the merits of the plan and at last agreed it might just work. By the time the Irishman returned to the manor, he was again a happy man.

"Have a safe journey, Colin." Moira blushed as the baron bent and kissed her under the watchful eye of Nigel Anson, who sat in a curricle. She knew the gesture was improper, but delighted in the sweetness of the moment all the same.

"We shall, my dear. Promise me you will be dressed in your finest gown when we return on Friday."

Moira smiled. "I promise."

Colin jumped up into the curricle and took his reins. With one last nod, he signaled the team into a brisk walk, guiding them out of the shelter of Montmoorland before he finally put them into a canter.

Watching the two men disappear round the bend in the drive, Moira jumped when her uncle's hand clamped down on her arm. "So there is only you and I for the next four days, lass."

Moira glanced at Uncle Sean and realized he was smiling for the first time since she'd told him of her engagement to Lord Lamont. But noting a sly gleam in his eyes, she felt a sudden wariness with her uncle for the first time in her life. "So it would seem, sir."

The gentleman chuckled as he led her back to the breakfast parlor. "Now don't be looking as if I were about to bite you, my dear. I've already had my breakfast this morning."

Moira laughed, giving up much of her suspicion as she fell into step with her relative.

"I merely have a suggestion I should like you to listen to." Sean Rourke had a great deal of confidence that he could talk nearly anyone into anything especially Moira, when he pulled the right heartstrings.

CHAPTER SIX

Four days later, Colin tooled his carriage up to the front of Montmoorland just after noon, anxious to again see Moira. With a tired and hungry Nigel trailing behind, he entered the manor shouting for Larkin to prepare a nuncheon. But instead of finding his butler, a smirking Harry stepped from the Yellow Salon.

"Lamont, Lady Ferries demands your presence within, at once."

"What is Grandmother doing here?" Uncertain how he felt about the old lady's arrival, Colin had no such doubts about his decision to marry Moira. Whatever the dowager decided about his choice of a wife, he believed that with Eire's Luck they would eventually be financially secure in the future.

"She has come to see your chosen bride, old fellow."

Colin knew he had his cousin to thank for that lady's unexpected arrival. There would be no avoiding a meeting with his grandmother. Before entering, he asked Nigel to inform Moira of their return. After his friend departed, he strolled toward the Yellow Salon.

As Harry turned to enter the room as well, Colin put out his hand, stopping him. "This is private, Cousin. Why not find something else to amuse yourself since you assured me your are so good at that?"

Harry looked as if he might protest his exclusion, but there was such a look in the baron's eyes that the dandy suddenly thought it safer elsewhere. With a slight nervous twitch to his thin lips, he asked, "Shall I ask your housekeeper to send refreshments? My great-aunt insisted on waiting until your return before partaking of any food."

"An excellent suggestion, Harry, and you might want to linger in the kitchen for a bit." Certain his edict would be followed, Colin entered the salon and shut the door behind him.

His grandmother reclined on a Charles II daybed of worn yellow damask, which she'd seen fit to draw near an open window. She wore a plain gray traveling gown, which was elegant and fashionable. Upon seeing her grandson she sat up.

"There you are. I have been left here idling for more than two hours awaiting you. I hope you know what an inconvenience this has been, being dragged halfway across the country due to one of your foolish starts.''

Colin strolled up and kissed the cheek Lady Ferries turned to him. "I haven't the least notion what you are referring to, Grandmother.''

"Don't take me for a flat, dear boy. I have twice your age and experience. Where is that creature?''

"I believe my cousin has gone to the kitchen to order us some refreshments.'' Colin smiled innocently at the lady.

"Don't be impertinent, my boy. You know of whom I speak. Harry tells me you have some scandalous Irish female and her horse staying here.''

"Well, actually, the horse is in the stables. As a rule, they don't make good houseguests.''

"Cease your levity at once, young man, and tell me if you are planning on—"

The door to the salon opened and Nigel entered, making straight for Colin. "I fear there is no one in the manor. Not Miss O'Donnell, nor Rourke, nor even Larkin.'' The gentleman paused a moment, then added, "And Eire's Luck is missing as well. Mrs. Jones said everyone departed some time during the morning, but she was busy in the stillroom and hasn't any notion where they went.''

Colin searched his mind for a reason for them all to have left. With a sinking feeling, he remembered that day was race day. Had Rourke somehow convinced Moira to ride that cursed stallion despite everything? Fear filled his heart at the thought of his beloved endangering herself in a race. He knew he had to stop her if he could.

"I must go to York at once. There can be little doubt where they have all gone if they took the stallion."

Nigel put his hand on the baron's arm. "But your horses are spent."

Colin knew his friend was right, for he'd pushed them hard to get back to Montmoorland early. Then he realized he needed a closed carriage if Moira was masquerading as a groom. "I shall use Grandmother's coach and team. I will need the privacy if a certain person has disobeyed my orders and donned masculine attire."

Nigel had been made aware of Moira's plan during the long trip to London and back. "Shall I come with you?"

"Stay and keep Lady Ferries entertained. If I make it in time, we shall return shortly."

Colin strode from the room without taking his leave of the occupants, his thoughts were so centered on saving Moira from this scandalous affair. He heard his grandmother demanding him to return at once, but he didn't have time to waste on explaining his actions. The race would be starting soon. He only prayed he could get there in time.

Knavesmire Racing Grounds, along with Doncaster, was one of the premier sites of the race world in the north of England. The spring race was held each year in May or June and attracted thousands of gentlemen throughout the land. Despite Colin's intentions, it took him nearly an hour to get close to the course, the roads being clogged with gentlemen in carriages

come to see the race. The event was well underway
by the time he arrived. In hopes of seeing what was
happening, he climbed up on the box of Lady Ferries's coach with her driver and watched as a field of
horses thundered toward the finish line.

He spied Eire's Luck leading the pack, Moira
hunched down low on the animal's back. Clods of dirt
flew and the horses galloped full tilt as they neared the
grandstand. A tightness filled Colin's chest, but he
was uncertain if it was anger at her or fear for her.
Why had she agreed to the ride when she knew he
fully intended to race the animal at a later date with
a proper jockey? No doubt, Sean Rourke had managed to coerce her into the dangerous step.

In truth, as his gaze swept over her, he had to admit
that, if he hadn't known who she was, he wouldn't
have been able to tell she was a female. She wore
loose garb that hid her feminine shape and a wide-
brimmed hat, which was nothing like the traditional
hat that jockeys wore. She looked like an ordinary
groom who'd taken the notion to ride the race.

While the competition drew near its end, Colin
began to hope it might be possible to get her away
after the race without causing a scandal. He held his
breath as the field of horses thundered past with
Eire's Luck well in front. He heard the horse's name
murmured throughout the throng of racing enthusiasts, but he didn't stop to hear what was being said.
Instead, he jumped down from the carriage and
pushed his way to where a crowd was beginning to
form around the winner. He peered through the
multitude of excited gentlemen and tried to see

Moira, but she'd already slid from the horse as it was
being led back toward the grandstand.

As he came up beside Lucky, he saw Sean Rourke
leading the stallion, accepting the congratulations of
the teeming crowd. Colin didn't take the time to dress
down the gentleman for getting his niece involved
in the race. Seeing the top of the battered round hat,
he grabbed Moira and shoved his way toward his
carriage, excusing his rudeness by saying the lad was
ill and must be taken home.

"Lord Lamont, Lord Lamont, come back. We must
speak." The Irishman's cry could barely be heard
above the excited babble, but Colin paid no heed to
the man who'd convinced Moira to go against his
wishes.

Colin could feel her struggling against his grasp,
but he was too angry with her at the moment to try
to converse. At last, they reached the carriage and
he shoved her in. He called to the driver to return
to Montmoorland at once, then climbed in, taking
the seat facing the lady.

Her head hung down so low, all Colin could see
was the top of the round black hat she wore. Didn't
she even have a notion of how badly she could have
been hurt had things gone wrong? The very thought
made him bark, "Why did you decide to race Eire's
Luck after we agreed to wait?"

Silence greeted his question. Colin tried to rein in
his temper. It was always his worst failing, and he
knew that Moira would never have done this on her
own. Rourke no doubt had pressured her. Colin suspected that without his support she'd probably felt

she had no choice. Believing her bashfulness a sign she was ashamed of her actions, Colin's tone softened. "I know your uncle can be quite persuasive, but I don't think that rogue had your best interest in mind when he convinced you to ride, my dear."

The carriage rocked along and still there was no response from beneath the wide brim. Filled with remorse for his temper, and only wanting her to throw herself into his arms, Colin spoke with a husky voice. "Can you forgive my anger, my dear? I shall blame it on my stomach, for I have not dined since breakfast and I am grouchy as a bear when I'm famished. When we get home, we shall share a good meal. Then I intend to take you to the vicarage and kiss you soundly when we are married."

A low Irish voice announced, "Sure I am that a meal sounds a bit all right, but I think the law forbids you from marryin' your groom."

Colin's mouth dropped open when the black hat was whisked away and Jim grinned at him from across the aisle.

At last Colin realized that Jim had ridden Eire's Luck. "But . . . I thought no one could ride that stallion but Moira."

Jim sat back, his grin widening. "Sure, the lady was always warnin' us grooms to stay away from Lucky, him bein' a bit too lively. But all that time I was sailin' to England, then takin' care of him at Warwick, he and I become friends like. Got to where he didn't fret when I come to his stall, so I tried to ride him while Miss Moira was ailin' and we took to one another like a tippler to ale."

Colin was flooded with relief that Moira hadn't been involved in the race. Jim would be perfect for handling the highbred horse. "How would you like a permanent job as Lucky's jockey, Jim?"

The lad sat up with a grin on his face. "With proper clothes and a lid?"

"Everything first-class, my boy." Colin smiled back.

"Sure, and it's every groom's dream, my lord."

Colin grew thoughtful. "Might I ask how you and Mr. Rourke were able to get Moira to agree to let you ride the horse?"

The new jockey looked sheepishly at his lordship. "The lady don't know what we was about, sir. Mr. Sean arranged for your butler to take her to York for a fancy new weddin' dress."

Wedding. The way things were going Colin wasn't certain they would have one that day, especially if his grandmother had anything to do with the matter. He fell silent after congratulating Jim on his feat. He prayed they would reach Montmoorland before Moria and Larkin returned. He didn't want her to face his grandmother's hostility alone.

They rode the rest of the way in silence. At last, they arrived at the manor, and Colin jumped down and hurried inside.

Larkin was hovering near the Yellow Salon as Colin entered the front hall. Colin knew at once that he was too late and prayed that his grandmother hadn't been rude to his fiancée. His gaze scanned the butler's face, but the old man's countenance was that unreadable mask servants present to their employers.

"Welcome home, my lord. The ladies await your pleasure in the Yellow Salon."

Colin knew that nothing his grandmother could say or do would stop him from marrying Moira. He loved Moira and was willing to sacrifice a fortune for the lady. With a determined set to his jaw, he opened the door, then halted in surprise. The two ladies sat before a tea table, heads together in genial conversation. When Moira spied him, she stood up, a smile of greeting on her beautiful face. She wore a lovely cream-colored silk gown trimmed with delicate Brussels lace and pale blue ribbons that matched her eyes. Tiny white roses had been worked into her reddish-blond curls. She looked an angel.

"You are here, sir." The words were spoken shyly.

Colin could only nod his head as he moved to where the ladies were, never removing his eyes from her. He was overwhelmed by her beauty. With an effort, he tugged his gaze from Moira and stared at his grandmother. She too had changed since his earlier encounter with her. At present, she wore an elegant purple taffeta gown and a simple white cap with purple ribbons.

But the most amazing thing she wore was a smile on her lined face. "Well, my boy, don't just stand there, gaping at your beautiful bride. Go and change your clothes. We have kept the vicar waiting long enough."

Still unable to believe his eyes and ears, Colin placed a possessive arm around Moira. "Grandmother, I thought you disapproved of my choice of a bride."

The elderly lady rose with surprising agility for someone near seventy. A frown settled on her face. "Nonsense. What I disapprove of is a young coxcomb coming to my home telling scandalous tales that prove to be entirely false, and so I told Harry when I sent him about his business. Your fiancée is delightful, a proper young lady. How can I fault you for marrying someone from Ireland for love, dear boy, when I did much the same thing myself years ago?"

Colin looked at Moira in amazement, then back to the dowager. "But you always told me your first husband was a fool."

The dowager nodded her head. "And so he was, dear boy. But that doesn't mean I didn't love him. 'Twas all long ago. What is important is here and now. In the past hour, I have discovered that Miss O'Donnell is just the young lady to make you happy. Now, before we leave for the vicarage, I must go retrieve my reticule and see what has happened to your friend, Anson. He went to dress and never returned. The boy must be a dandy."

Colin chuckled. "Nigel would take great offense at being called such. He fashions himself a Corinthian."

Lady Ferries shrugged. "All you young men try to cut a dash in one way or the other. Perchance the fellow was merely leaving Miss O'Donnell and me alone to get acquainted. No doubt, the pair of you would like a moment alone as well without an interfering old woman."

When Colin and Moira tried to protest her referring to herself in such a manner, Lady Ferries stopped them. "Oh, I know what I am, my dears. You needn't toady to me. I've had enough of that from Harry over the past four days to last for the next fifty years." Saying that, the dowager exited the salon.

Colin smiled at his fiancée, then crushed her to him in a passionate kiss. Reluctantly drawing away, he said, "I must go up and change. We cannot keep Grandmother waiting for the ceremony any longer." He hesitated a moment, then stroked Moira's cheek with his finger. "Are you still certain that this hasty wedding is to your taste, my love? I don't think the dowager would object to our waiting until we could send for your family."

Moira, still in the throes of her feelings from the searing kiss, knew she didn't want to wait the months it would take to bring her mother and sisters to England. She wanted to be Colin's wife this very day.

"I am ready to be wed. Uncle Sean is all the family I need at my wedding." Then the lady frowned. "Where is Uncle Sean? I have not seen him since I returned. Has he gotten into trouble again?"

"In a manner of speaking." Colin smiled and quickly told her the tale of the race and Jim. Moira was delighted, yet deep within her was a sense of disappointment that she hadn't been there to witness Lucky's triumph. "I wish I had been there."

"He can run next month at Ascot. I promise to escort you, but first I am taking you to the vicarage and making you mine."

Moira saw the ardent look in Colin's amber eyes, and as his lips covered hers, she forgot about all but the man who stood before her and her desire to be his.

ABOUT THE AUTHOR

Lynn Collum lives with her family in DeLand, FL, and is the author of three previous Zebra Regency romances: *A Game of Chance, Elizabeth and the Major,* and *The Spy's Bride.* She is currently working on her next Zebra Regency romance, *Lady Miranda's Masquerade,* which will be published in June, 1999. Lynn loves hearing from her readers and you may write to her c/o Zebra Books. Please include a self-addressed stamped envelope if you wish a response.

THE HEIRESS BRIDE

MONA GEDNEY

Icy gusts of wind tossed the carriage from side to side so that it seemed to Alexa that she was in a ship rather than in a four-wheeled vehicle firmly attached to the earth. Despite her lap robe, she shivered a little, for the warm bricks at her feet had long ago become as cold as the floorboards. Even though she had no real desire to reach her destination, she began to feel that anything might be preferable to the cold and the incessant rolling of the coach.

Some might suppose that being orphaned at sixteen and abandoned to the none too tender mercies of an elderly distant cousin must automatically spell misery for the young person in question. Despite her unhappy situation, however, Alexa Howard was nothing if not resilient and resourceful, and she had not the slightest intention of remaining miserable.

That was an intention that she had had to remind herself of as she had said good-bye to the household staff she had known all her life and driven away from her home, which was soon to be sold. The bleak winter day seemed to suit her mood all too well, and it was with some trouble that Alexa remembered her father's advice always to go over rough ground as lightly as possible. She knew that she would be grieving over the loss of her parents for many a long year, but she knew, too, that they would not have expected her to make a spectacle of her mourning. They had both firmly believed in putting the best face on any situation, no matter how grim. The Howards did not burden others with their problems.

As Alexa's carriage approached Lathrop Hall, she wiped her eyes, sat up a little straighter, and slipped her hand inside her pelisse to clutch the gold locket that held the minatures of her parents. Already they seemed very far away from her, even farther than they had the day of the funeral, when she had walked behind their coffins to the church for the service and then to the sunny churchyard to watch them laid to rest. She had resented that bright autumn sunlight, which had seemed to mock her desolation. The present day's bleakness seemed far more suitable to her mood.

For a moment, she closed her eyes and pictured them as she had seen them last, both dark haired and bright eyed and merry, waving good-bye to her from their carriage window for as long as they could see her. Their leavetaking had been lighthearted because their journey to Liverpool was for the purpose of meeting with a young sea captain who would restore their fortune, which had literally gone up in flames twice that year: once, when the huge London warehouse that housed their import business burned, destroying everything, and again, when their sugar plantation in Barbados met the same fate during a slave revolt that shook the island.

Despite the fact that their livelihood was gone, the Howards had remained optimistic, certain that something would turn up. And something soon had. A young captain who had transported their sugarcane upon several occasions wrote to Gerald Howard, offering him the opportunity to invest in his undertaking. With his ship loaded with trinkets and dry goods, Captain Derringer planned to sail round Cape Horn to the Pacific coast of North America to trade with the Indians for furs. He had had the good fortune to meet a man familiar with that part of the world who would sail with him and guide him to their customers when they arrived.

Her father, always a gambler at heart, had agreed to use the last of their savings to finance the voyage, pointing out that beaver hats were still in vogue. "It will remake our fortune," he had assured his wife and daughter.

Alexa smiled sadly as she remembered their exuberant confidence in the young captain's plans. They would not allow themselves to consider the possibility that his venture might fail.

"Bad things come in threes," her mother had always said, but she had made no mention of that after their two financial disasters, apparently choosing not to invite misfortune. Two bad things had happened so far, Alexa had known—the loss of the warehouse and the plantation. Perhaps, she had thought, the pattern was different that time, and they were to be canceled out by a third thing that was good—the voyage. Jeanette Howard, who thought that her husband could do no wrong, had agreed to the investment and had assured Alexa that they would soon be back from Liverpool with their fortunes all but made. They would have only to wait for Captain Derringer's return from North America.

It was after her parents' meeting with the captain that the third bad thing had indeed happened—and it was far worse than Alexa could ever have imagined. The inn where her parents were staying in Liverpool had caught fire late one night and burned to the ground, killing over half of the guests, among them her parents.

Their solicitor, a dry little man named Lewis Lawrence, had brought her the terrible news. When he arrived, Alexa had at first thought it no more than one of his ordinary business visits. However, when he had spoken very gravely and asked to see her with her governess, she had begun to have misgivings. Nothing, though, had prepared her for the emotional wrench that gripped her when he had reluctantly given her the news of her parents' deaths.

The grief of losing her beloved parents had at first deadened the shock of realizing that she was truly all alone in the world and that her parents had left her very little money with which to face the future. Mr. Lawrence had explained matters as kindly and simply as possible, and it had been he who had let the servants go, including her governess, and he who had made arrangements to sell her home, saving every penny that he could so that he could return it to Alexa.

It had also been he who had corresponded with Mrs. Lavinia Lathrop, the widow of Sterling Lathrop, who had been a distant cousin of her mother. After an exchange of letters and a visit to her home in distant Sussex, the little solicitor had made arrangements for Alexa to be Mrs. Lathrop's companion until she came of age at twenty-one, at which time she would receive her inheritance from her parents. The inheritance, he had sadly informed her, would be quite small, due to the unfortunate occurrences of the past year. Still, it would be enough for a young woman to use as a dowry. He did not add that her choice of husband would be quite limited, given her severely straitened circumstances.

When the carriage drew to a halt in front of Lathrop Hall, Alexa allowed herself to be helped down by the footman, her head erect and her eyes bright. She had not the slightest intention of entering the Hall as a poor relative, one who would be living upon charity from her well-to-do relative. Since her father had been in trade, she knew that her mother's family had looked down upon him—and upon her mother for marrying him. Even this unknown distant cousin, all that was left of her mother's family, would undoubtedly be familiar with the details of that social disgrace.

Her expression calm and her back straight, Alexa had assessed her situation carefully from the moment she entered the Hall. The butler, she noted, had a red nose and was slightly inclined to weave as he led her into the drawing room to meet his mistress. Nor did her quick eyes miss the layer of dust on the furniture and the lack of luster in the wood floors—clear evidence of careless housekeeping and servants who did not take their work seriously.

When she met her new guardian, Mrs. Lavinia Lathrop, she realized the reason for the servants' casual attitude. Mrs. Lathrop reclined upon a velvet sofa, a cold cloth pressed to her brow, while a tiny maid waved burnt feathers beneath her nose.

"Oh, my! So you are little Alexa—you unfortunate child," moaned Mrs. Lathrop, raising her head for just a moment to inspect the newcomer. "Almost as unfortunate as your poor mother."

Collapsing once more, she moaned, "Fetch me my sal volatile at once!" to the little maid, who promptly scuttled from the room.

"What is wrong, Mrs. Lathrop?" inquired Alexa, her eyes wide. "Have you been taken ill?"

Mrs. Lathrop, a fragile woman with silvery hair and sharp blue eyes, glanced up at her guest in astonishment. "Taken ill?" she asked blankly. "No indeed, poor child. Why, I have *been* ill for years! Did you not know it? Did Mr. Lawrence not tell you so?"

"He did not," replied Alexa, her tone apologetic. Mrs. Lathrop was clearly very proud of her delicate health. "Perhaps he had too much to deal with at the time to remember to tell me that. I'm certain that he considered your situation a grave one, though.

Do tell me what I might do to make you more comfortable.''

Mrs. Lathrop raised herself upon an elbow to regard the newcomer with a more favorable eye. All too often people—her own children among them— were not inclined to take her illnesses seriously.

"I don't know, dear child," she moaned. "I seem to have trouble taking in everything that is happening around me. Sometimes I feel that there is a wall of glass between me and my servants and that they cannot hear me."

Thinking grimly of the laxness she had already noted, Alexa removed her pelisse, handed it to the butler, and replied briskly, "Pray don't trouble yourself at all, ma'am. I shall see to everything."

And see to it she did. Before anyone, including Mrs. Lathrop, quite knew what was happening, Alexa had rung for the housekeeper, called that lady's attention to the dust collecting upon everything and noted that it could not be healthy for an invalid like Mrs. Lathrop, and when the little maid reappeared with the *sal volatile*, she was dispatched to the cook with instructions to return with a cup of nourishing chicken broth for her mistress. Deeply gratified by such attention to her comfort, Mrs. Lathrop sank back upon her sofa and allowed herself to be cosseted.

Having set things momentarily to rights, Alexa devoted the next few days to inspecting Lathrop Hall very closely, discovering that what she had immediately suspected was all too true. Her sickly guardian had a large but inefficient staff and absolutely no interest in managing them. When Alexa tactfully suggested that, in the role of companion, she might be able to execute some of the household duties that Mrs. Lathrop was too ill to manage, the lady indicated her willingness to have her do so by granting her *carte blanche* in the handling of household affairs.

Once she was certain of her ground, Alexa immediately settled in and took charge. The butler, who had spent the better part of each day sampling the wares in the wine cellar, and the slovenly houskeeper, who had lined her purse at the expense of her employer, were dismissed immediately, new ones were engaged, and Alexa ruled the household with a firm hand. In the months that followed, she found, as had many before her, that keeping one's time fully occupied helped in learning to live with grief.

Years of helping her gentle mother in their London home had given her a competence and self-assurance far beyond her years, so she was soon able to make a decided difference in Mrs. Lathrop's comfort. Indeed, it was not long before her grateful guardian could no longer recall what life without Alexa had been like.

"As long as I am alive, you need never fear, child," she told Alexa reassuringly some six months after her arrival. "You have a home at Lathrop Hall for as long as you wish it, and I shall leave you enough in my will to be certain that you will be able to care for yourself when I am gone."

"You are very good, ma'am," replied Alexa sincerely, "but you need not be troubled about me. Something will turn up."

Despite her parents' unfortunate deaths, their optimistic view of life remained firmly rooted in her. Grateful though she was to Mrs. Lathrop for taking her in, Alexa had not the slightest intention of living out her life as a lady's companion, dwindling from girlhood to spinsterhood in the same quiet household. She was not certain just how she would manage it, but she had every intention of living her life in a far more interesting manner.

And, before her first year at Lathrop Hall was over, she discovered that she would have the means to do so. Captain Derringer presented himself, along with Mr. Lawrence, to inform her that her father's investment in the voyage had repaid him many times over. The captain had sailed the morning before the fire and had only learned of the unhappy fate of his patrons upon his return to England.

"You are quite secure now, Miss Howard," Mr. Lawrence assured her. "If I had known that you would receive this much of a return upon your father's investment, I would not have insisted upon selling your home and settling you here."

He regarded Alexa with a troubled glance. "I can't tell you, ma'am, how sorry I am to have displaced you when it was not necessary."

Alexa smiled at him. "You did the right thing for me, sir," she assured him. "Had I remained at home, I could have only been reminded of my loss, and I would have had little enough to occupy my mind. Here I have found problems to solve and a relative who has needed my help."

"You are kind to try to set my mind at rest," murmured Mr. Lawrence. "Do you not wish for your own

establishment now that you can afford it? I could
find a gentlewoman who would live with you as a
chaperon.''

Alexa shook her head. ''I have a home here for
the time being—and I am needed. What I should like,
though,'' she added, smiling at Captain Derringer,
''is the opportunity to invest in the captain's next
business venture.''

Derringer bowed and returned her smile. ''Your
vote of confidence is greatly appreciated, ma'am. I
shall not let you down.''

Nor did he. Alexa invested in his next three voyages,
all of which were successful and greatly increased
her fortune. After Mr. Lawrence's first visit with the
captain, the knowlege that she had an independent
fortune and was not a drain upon Mrs. Lathrop was
an added source of security and encouraged her independent nature. She now had her own income and
would come into her fortune on her twenty-first birthday or upon the day of her marriage, whichever came
first. Her own plan was to take a house in London
upon the occasion of that twenty-first birthday. She
had no immediate desire to leave Mrs. Lathrop, who
she felt would be helpless without her. So she devoted
her time to running that lady's household and keeping her company.

When she was twenty, Mrs. Lathrop reluctantly dis-
pensed with her companionship for several weeks so
that Alexa could accompany her guardian's favorite
granddaughter to London for her introduction to
the *ton*. Alexa had expected no Season of her own
because of her own regrettable ties to trade, but it

appeared that she would now have an opportunity to see society. And, she decided, it would be the opportune moment to look for that house. Her twenty-first birthday, on the twenty-fifth of June was rapidly approaching.

"Keep a close eye upon Lily," Mrs. Lathrop instructed her, "for goodness knows that stepmother of hers won't. She means to marry the child to the first comer—and I don't want my granddaughter to have her head turned by some man-milliner thrown in her path. If you go with her, I can be certain that someone has Lily's best interests at heart."

"I will do my best," Alexa assured her. "You have been too kind to me for me to do otherwise."

Mrs. Lathrop looked at Alexa closely for a moment, then smiled. "I know, my dear, just what you have done to make my life easier, and don't think for a moment I don't appreciate it. And I know how much you are looking forward to living in London yourself, but if I could do something to keep you here with me at Lathrop Hall, I would do it in an instant."

She sighed, knowing full well that there was nothing she could do. Then she added firmly, "I want Lily to be happy. Neither of her parents has the least notion of what that means—but I want you to guide her, Alexa. Heaven knows that you have mind and will enough for fourteen people."

Lily was an exceptionally pretty young woman—and she would eventually inherit a large portion of her grandmother's fortune—but not even Mrs. Lathrop considered her particularly bright. In short, she would be the quarry of every London Lothario seeking a wealthy bride. Alexa would have her hands full, she knew, but she was looking forward to her trip, nonetheless. As she packed, she began once again to imagine what her own life would be like when she came of age and became mistress of her own life.

"Well, I'm sure that I don't understand why Grandmother insisted upon having you come to Town with me," said Lily crossly as Alexa helped her to dress her hair for their first evening in London. "After all, I have Papa and Louisa—why should I have to have you, too? It's *my* Season, after all!"

"Of course it is," Alexa assured her patiently. Mrs. Lathrop had very wisely not told her granddaughter just why Alexa was to accompany her, understanding very well that Lily would take exception to having a watchdog with her. She had not considered the fact that Lily, selfish to the bone, might object to sharing her trip to London in any way. "This trip is entirely for you, Lily. Your grandmother was just trying to be kind to me. She knows how I've longed to come back to London."

"I thought you were from Sussex," Lily replied, pulling impatiently at a stubborn curl and biting her lips to make them redder. "Why do you speak of coming back to London?"

"We lived in Sussex most of the year, but my parents had a house in London, too, and I always looked forward to being here."

"Of course, you know that even if your parents had lived, you could never have had a Season of your own, Alexa,'' Lily pointed out for the fifth time that evening. ''The only reason that you are being invited to everything now is because of me.''

''Yes, I know that,'' Alexa responded cheerfully, keeping her mind focused on Mrs. Lathrop's kindness so that she would not be tempted to respond in kind. ''So isn't it fortunate that I have no real interest in being a member of the *ton*?''

''I suppose that you are trying to say that you will find all of this tremendously boring,'' Lily returned, her disbelief obvious.

''Well, I can't say that, can I?'' Alexa said. ''As yet I haven't sampled any of the life of polite Society. Tonight's rout will be my first.''

''And mine,'' Lily replied. ''And I intend to catch the eye of every man there.'' Her voice was filled with satisfaction as she surveyed herself in the cheval glass, pirouetting to catch the full effect of her clinging white silk gown. ''Isn't it fortunate that brunettes are all the rage?''

''Indeed, it is,'' agreed Alexa, who did not begrudge Lily a moment of her pleasure. The girl was indeed a vision of loveliness, and her dark beauty was certainly much more dramatic than that of Alexa, whose bright brown hair seemed much less glamorous when compared to Lily's midnight curls. ''I'm certain that you will capture the hearts of half the men present tonight.''

''Only half?'' pouted Lily, her question serious rather than humorous.

Recognizing that, Alexa hastily amended her statement. ''What could I have been thinking? Undoubtedly every manly heart there will be laid at your feet, Lily, and the women will all be wild with jealousy."

"Do you really think so?" purred Lily, still inspecting her reflection closely.

Alexa, who was only just realizing that Lily had no sense of humor at all, nodded solemnly. There could be no glint of laughter in her voice or her eyes, lest Lily should take a pet. She had begun to suspect that taking care of Mrs. Lathrop's granddaughter was going to be much more trying than she had at first realized. Invalid though she was, Mrs. Lathrop had normally traveled to her son's home for her visits with his family, for they had indicated that such an arrangement was much more convenient for them. Because of this, Alexa had had little direct contact with the girl until then—and it appeared that she had a challenge on her hands.

The party that evening confirmed her suspicion. Lily flirted audaciously with every male who came within her range, whether he was a graybeard or a stripling. Alexa did her best to keep an eye on Lily without appearing to do so, but it was a trying ordeal. Lily's behavior was outrageous, for she laughed too loudly and flirted too brazenly, and Alexa, realizing that neither her stepmother nor her father would do anything to curb her behavior, was at first at a loss as to how to handle the matter. Then she remembered Almack's.

"You know, my dear, I noticed that a few of the ladies in the corner were watching your flirtation with Lord Darrowby just now," she told Lily when that young lady came over to her for help in pinning up a tear in her train.

"Spiteful old cats!" Lily responded elegantly.

"They may be," Alexa returned cautiously, "but I'm afraid that one or two of them might be rather powerful old cats. It would do you no good, you know, to be denied a voucher for Almack's."

"Why should I care about that?" asked Lily, yawning. "What is so special about Almack's?"

"Simply that everyone who is anyone is received there," replied Alexa casually, studying the tear in the train rather than Lily's expression. "Not to be received at Almack's is the kiss of death for a young woman wishing to make her mark on London Society."

Lily stared at her, wide-eyed. "What do any of those old cats have to do with that?" she demanded, staring at the group of ladies under discussion.

"It is something of a mistake to call them all old cats," returned Alexa. "I think you should be a little more cautious in your choice of words, Lily, for someone might overhear you."

"Why should I care about that?" asked Lily.

"Firstly, because not all of them are old—you should look at them more closely—and secondly, because one of them is Lady Jersey, who is one of the patronesses of Almack's."

"Is she indeed?" asked Lily, her eyes wider than ever.

Alexa nodded solemnly. "To make Sally Jersey dislike you would be one of the most careless things you could do, Lily, for they say that she has a wicked tongue. She would use it against you if you were to make her dislike you."

"Well, she won't dislike me!" announced Lily resolutely.

"Indeed?" inquired Alexa smoothly. "And what if someone overheard you calling her an old cat? Perhaps you've already destroyed your chances."

Lily bit her lip and glanced over her shoulder a little nervously, surveying the crowd and trying to see if anyone was looking at her accusingly. Alexa noted with satisfaction that her words had hit home, for her charge was no longer inclined to effect such a careless, mannerless attitude. She was certain that Lily would soon return to her normal demeanor, but for the moment at least, Alexa had the advantage and she pressed it.

"You must remember, Lily, that your behavior is being studied closely even when you are not aware of it. You would not wish to be barred from some very desirable events simply because you did something careless or let your tongue run away with you."

Lily swallowed hard and nodded, her eyes still flying nervously from face to face in the surrounding throng. Fortunately, a young man came to claim her hand for the next dance, and Lily took his arm quietly, allowing him to lead her out onto the floor in a most unexceptionable and ladylike manner.

"I congratulate you, ma'am. That was a most impressive performance," said a deep, lazy voice close to Alexa's shoulder, and she wheeled about to face a tall, dark man, his eyes as filled with mockery as his voice. "Are you thinking of becoming a preacher in one of those little chapels that are springing up in the countryside? You would be quite good at it, I think. All the young ladies would wish to hear your strictures on proper decorum and the young men—well, the young men would come just to look at you, you know.''

"Do you make it a habit to eavesdrop, sir?" Alexa inquired briskly, turning away from him and giving her attention to Lily. "I could deliver a brief sermon on that evil as well.''

Her tormentor chuckled unrepentantly. "I am certain that you could—and I should be delighted to hear your thoughts on the subject. Could I persuade you to join me in a glass of champagne? No, no," he added hastily, not waiting for her reply, "forgive me, ma'am. I wasn't thinking. Would you join me instead for a cup of lemonade or orange squash? I realize that a lady like yourself would not indulge in strong drink.''

Thoroughly irritated, Alexa replied tartly, "I would enjoy a glass of champagne, sir, if it is of good quality and very dry. Otherwise, I should prefer water.''

The gentleman executed a deep bow, still smiling. "If the champagne does not meet your standards, ma'am, I shall make it my business to find a suitable substitute. Our hostess's wine cellar is well known to me, and I am certain that I would be able to procure something that would meet your very exacting standards.''

Alexa inclined her head slightly in acknowledgment of his remark, and ignored the twinkle in his eye as he murmured, "Such a very interesting twist, if you will forgive my saying so, ma'am. I had no notion that Methodists were also connoisseurs of wine."

As the stranger left on his errand, Alexa glanced about for a place to be seated and found a small table tucked away behind the palms where her eavesdropper had been lurking. When he returned, he found her there, tapping one small sandaled foot impatiently while she watched Lily from her hidden position. Fortunately, the girl was still behaving herself very well.

"Still playing propriety, ma'am?" inquired the gentleman, who carried two glasses of champagne and was followed by a waiter with two plates heaped with delicacies from one of the tables in the adjoining room. "It appears that your charge is doing very nicely without your gimlet eyes upon her."

"For the moment," Alexa replied grimly, accepting her plate with a brief smile and thank-you for the waiter and no smile and an extremely brief thank-you for the gentleman.

"Tsk, tsk," he murmured, seating himself and stretching out his long legs casually to make himself more comfortable. "If you are to set an example of manners, ma'am, you will have to do better than this."

Lifting his glass of champagne, he said, "To your health, Miss—" He suddenly broke off, smiling apologetically, as though he had forgotten something. "Forgive me, but I don't believe that we have met, ma'am. As a result, I don't know your name."

"And if you're wise, miss, you will not give it to

him," a woman said coldly. "You will be much happier if you never know the gentleman."

Startled, both Alexa and the stranger glanced up. A tall, slender young woman was standing next to them, her disapproval almost tangible. The palms had sheltered her approach from their view.

"Why, Marian. Why ever would you make such an unkind comment?" the gentleman reproachfully said. "What will Miss . . . Miss . . ." He looked hopefully at Alexa, waiting for her to fill in her name.

"Howard," said Alexa reluctantly.

"What will Miss Howard think of me?" he finished.

"She will think that Lord Rivington is precisely what everyone says that he is: a rake who cannot be trusted with women," replied the young woman, no smile or playful tone softening her words.

Before either of the others could respond, a new voice answered her. "You must remember, however, Miss Howard, that Marian has been throwing herself in Lord Rivington's path ever since her coming out two years ago. Since he has never paid the slightest attention to her, she has become bitter."

Another young lady, one with laughter in her eyes and in her voice, had joined them in their leafy retreat. The young woman named Marian glared at the newcomer and stalked off to the other side of the room.

"You must forgive Marian," the newcomer said to Alexa. "She is inclined to be a little too possessive— particularly with people that have never belonged to her." Smiling at Lord Rivington, she gave a brief curtsy. "Do come to see us soon, Robert," she said and disappeared as suddenly as she had come.

"What a very charming young woman," said Alexa, looking after her thoughtfully. "She is a pronounced contrast to the first one."

"She is indeed," agreed Lord Rivington. "I am pleased, Miss Howard, that you approve of my sister. Perhaps that will make you look more kindly upon me."

"Your sister?" repeated Alexa, startled. The two were a sharp contrast in appearance: Lord Rivington tall and dark; his sister rather small with blue eyes and downy yellow hair. "I never would have suspected such a thing."

"I suspect that I cannot consider that a compliment, Miss Howard, since you seemed quite taken with Sophia. I do think," he added reproachfully, "that you could be a little more tactful. I might be quite cut up by your attitude, you know."

Alexa blushed, but with irritation, not embarrassment. "I believe that you are quite unaffected by my attitude, sir," she said stiffly. "In truth, I was thinking of the contrast in your physical appearances, but I do see that your personalities are strikingly dissimilar as well. Your sister has very pretty manners."

Lord Rivington's dark eyebrows rose. "And I see, Miss Howard, that you feel no compunction whatsoever about cutting me to the quick."

"I am sure that it is not in my power to do any such thing, Lord Rivington," she said, rising so that she could move to a vantage point where she could see Lily more clearly and where she could be free of her unwanted company. "And I am growing weary of providing you with your sport for the evening. I suggest that you single out another unfortunate and render her life uncomfortable. I am certain that Miss—Marian—would be more than willing to be the object of your attentions."

"But, Miss Howard," said Lord Rivington reproachfully, "I don't wish to direct my attentions elsewhere. I thought that you and I had come to an understanding."

Alexa looked at him indignantly. "We have done no such thing, Lord Rivington, as you very well know."

He bowed, his eyes still merry, although his tone was serious. "Then I fear that I have failed in my efforts, ma'am. I was hoping to do so. Having never before met such an extremely proper young woman, I felt that I might profit from a closer acqaintance, but I see that asking you to dance would be offensive to you. Forgive me for intruding upon you, ma'am." Then, he turned and made his way toward the cardroom.

Alexa felt suddenly bereft. He had been irritating enough, it was true, but he had been company. Without him, she felt exposed to the rest of the assemblage as she stood alone, still watching Lily dance.

That was not long the case, however. She was very soon joined by a pleasant-faced young man who introduced himself as Philip Forest, Lord Rivington's secretary.

"I know that you are new to London, Miss Howard, and I trust that Lord Rivington's conversation hasn't made you uncomfortable. I saw him speaking with you, and I'm afraid that he is greatly inclined to tease."

"It's kind of you to inquire, Mr. Forest. It's certainly true that Lord Rivington's manner is most unusual, but you shouldn't have to take responsibility for his actions. He is quite capable of doing so himself."

The young man nodded his head, smiling. "Oh, more than capable. But he is quite a charming man, you know—and a very generous one when he is able to be so. I feel very fortunate to be in his employ."

Alexa looked at Philip thoughtfully. He seemed an intelligent, pleasant man. She thought reluctantly that it spoke well for Rivington that his secretary thought so highly of him.

"How did you come to work for him?" Alexa inquired, then flushed furiously. "Never mind. Forgive me for inquiring into what is none of my business."

"Oh, but I don't mind telling you since it is to his credit," he responded, still smiling. "It does one no good, you see, to be born into a noble family if it is a large one without adequate fortune to support all of the children. In short, I found that I needed to support myself. And it was Lord Rivington who offered me a job—out of kindness, I believe, more than out of a need for a secretary. I have little enough to do for him, but I still earn a respectable salary."

"Somehow I would not have imagined his doing such a thing out of kindness," Alexa said thoughtfully. Lord Rivington's manner certainly had not revealed the slightest hint of a charitable nature.

"You may take my word for it, Miss Howard," Forest

replied. "He is a most unusual man. Don't be taken in by his facade."

Their interesting conversation was interrupted by the return of Lily at the close of her dance, and Alexa introduced her to Mr. Forest, who was clearly taken with her. Lily, who had no interest in a penniless young nobody, no matter how pleasant his manner and appearance, paid little attention to him and waved blithely to Alexa as her next partner bore her away.

"I see that we find ourselves in the same predicament, Miss Howard," Forest said, offering her his arm. "Would you do me the honor of dancing with me?"

"I would be delighted," she replied with sincerity, deciding that she could watch her charge from the dance floor just as well as she could from its side. And it was a pleasure to spend the next half hour with a well-mannered, intelligent young man who conversed as well as he danced. All in all, Alexa was regretful when the music came to an end.

"It's nice that you got to dance," Lily said graciously, fanning herself as she rejoined Alexa at the table among the palms. "And that young man was, of course, a very suitable partner since he really has no place here either. I understand that he is secretary to Lord Rivington."

"Mr. Forest is from a very good family," Alexa said briskly. "His grandfather is an earl, and it is no fault of Mr. Forest's if he is the youngest of a large family."

Lily shrugged, her lack of interest in the subject abundantly clear. "He still has no prospects," she observed, "so it all comes to the same thing in the end."

Lily finished her lemonade and rose as her next partner approached. She had not smiled during her conversation with Alexa, but now she wore an angelic expression, a smile softening her face so becomingly that Alexa could not blame the young man for staring down at her with delight. Whoever married Lily would have the opportunity to find out just what lay under that angelic exterior after the ceremony was over with and real life had begun. Alexa sighed, thinking of it. She hoped that the groom wouldn't be anyone that she liked. It would be hard to watch such a man go to his doom.

"I had thought that perhaps, being so strict in your views, you did not dance, ma'am, but I noticed that you stood up with my secretary for the last set."

Alexa looked up once more into the bright mocking eyes of Lord Rivington. "I am afraid that you leap to far too many conclusions about me, sir. As you say, I do dance."

"Would you give me the pleasure of this dance then, Miss Howard?" he asked, bowing low.

She shook her head. "Mr. Forest was a charming partner. I fear, however, that his employer would take advantage of the dance to pluck at me once again."

Lord Rivington chuckled. "You make it sound as though I have the disposition of a fishwife, ma'am. I assure you that I do not pluck at my dancing partners. I should hate to be responsible for making them forget just what they were about so that we came to grief on the dance floor."

"I am well aware that you are still making light of me, Lord Rivington," said Alexa stiffly. "I am amazed that a man of Mr. Forest's good breeding should think so highly of you."

As soon as the words had crossed her lips, she regretted them. She was rapidly becoming as rag mannered as Lily—and all because of the abominable man who was laughing at her for saying such a thing.

"I beg your pardon, sir," she said stiffly, avoiding his eyes. "I naturally don't know either of you well enough to make such a judgment, and even if I did, I certainly should not be giving voice to it."

"Oh, but you are painfully accurate, Miss Howard," he returned, placing a finger carelessly under her chin so that she was forced to look up at him. "And why should you not give voice to your opinion?"

"Because such a comment shows a want of good breeding," she replied sharply. Then her eyes flew across the floor to Lily, whom she had momentarily forgotten. "And because—"

"Because you are attempting to instill that good breeding into the lovely thing you have been hovering over all evening?" he finished, following her glance.

"No, of course not! I am merely her companion."

"Ah," he murmured. "I begin to see the situation. Poor Miss Howard. And why should you—who are also young and lovely—have to give your youth away as a companion? It is an unkind world."

"You are ridiculous, sir!" she snapped, snatching back the hand he had taken and raised to his lips. "Save your pity for someone who is in need of it. I am not!"

Wheeling away from him—and narrowly avoiding a palm—she marched away to another vantage point in the room and seated herself carefully next to a brood of fluttering older women, where she felt she would be fairly secure from Lord Rivington's attentions.

He is just like a cruel boy who has found a squirrel or a rabbit to torment! she thought to herself angrily. *Except that in this case the helpless creature is not as helpless as he thinks!*

"You do very well to keep your distance from Rivington, my dear."

Startled, Alexa looked up to see a little gray-haired woman with sharp eyes regarding her approvingly.

"I beg your pardon, ma'am," stammered Alexa, momentarily caught off guard. "Have we met?" She knew, of course, as did the lady, that they had not.

The speaker smiled at her. "I am Eustacia Draycourt, my dear. And what is your name?"

"Alexa Howard," she responded, looking once more at Lily. "I am here with Mr. and Mrs. Reginald Lathrop and their daughter." Lily's father was firmly ensconced in the cardroom, she knew, and heaven only knew where her stepmother was.

"I see," said Mrs. Draycourt, following her glance. "And that is Miss Lathrop?"

Alexa nodded.

"She is a beautiful young woman—as are you yourself, my dear, as Rivington noticed."

Together they watched Lily dancing for a moment, and Alexa was horrified to see that her partner had been replaced. She was now dancing with Lord Rivington.

Mrs. Draycourt turned to look at Alexa. "That is not a good thing," she said, lowering her voice discreetly. "Rivington is a very charming man, but he intends to marry an heiress, you know. If your friend has a fortune, she is in danger. If she does not, her heart is in danger."

"I had not noticed that he is particularly charming, Mrs. Draycourt, so I daresay Lily's heart is safe enough," Alexa replied with more ease than she felt.

"Not if he decides to marry her, which he might very well do if she has fortune enough," Mrs. Draycourt said frankly. "I would not be so open with you, my dear, since we are strangers to one another but I noticed you earlier in the evening and I saw that you were trying to guide Miss Lathrop, even though you are very young yourself. I thought that I should warn you about Rivington when I saw him with you. I should hate to see you come to grief."

"Thank you, ma'am. It's very kind of you," Alexa returned, still watching the pair on the dance floor.

"Not at all," said Mrs. Draycourt. "Although now I see that it is your young friend who is in danger of falling prey to his charm."

"No," said Alexa decisively, "I won't allow that to happen. When Lily marries, it will be to someone who will make her happy."

"Well, that wouldn't be Rivington. He has left behind a trail of broken hearts, and I'm sure his own wife will fare no better. He's never been with one woman longer than a year."

"Has he never been married then?" Alexa asked, suddenly curious. "He seems quite old to be a bachelor."

"So many another young woman has thought to her sorrow, my dear," said Mrs. Draycourt, shaking her head. "He has never been married, but he *has* had more love affairs than is decent, kept bad company, and gambled away a fortune. In short, he has done everything he wasn't supposed to do, and he has succeeded in charming the majority of London Society while he has done it."

Alexa sniffed. It seemed to her that London Society was all too easily charmed. Nonetheless, as she warily watched Rivington dance with Lily, she could see that he was making an impression on the girl. She was fluttering her eyelashes and glancing up at him provocatively—and most tellingly of all, she appeared to be making an effort to be less forward. Alexa would have to see to it that Lily found some other gentlemen to focus her attention upon. Lily was no match—in any way—for Rivington.

Alexa's fears proved to be well-founded. Lily could talk of no one else on the ride home that evening. Her father and stepmother scarcely listened to a word, being more caught up in their own memories of the evening, but hearing that Lily was infatuated by a man of the nobility, Reginald Lathrop merely nodded his head in approval. At least his daughter was selective.

"I thought that Philip Forest seemed a very fine young man," Alexa said at last, weary of hearing Lord Rivington's praises sung.

"He's all very well for someone like you, Alexa," Lily said graciously. "He is quiet and rather dull, as one would expect a secretary to be. But I need a man of wit and sophistication."

"A man like Rivington," Alexa finished for her, her tone dry.

"Exactly! I don't see how I can bear to wait until tomorrow morning to see him again!"

"I daresay you will manage," Alexa replied, her tone dryer still.

"What an old stick you are, Alexa! You have no feelings, no warm blood flowing through your veins! Rivington is right. You do have ice water in your veins instead of warm red blood."

Alexa, who had been thinking that such a passionate remark seemed out of character for Lily, sat upright suddenly, her eyes bright.

"I might have known it! It is Rivington who was feeding you these thoughts!" she exclaimed. "And so he thinks that I have ice water coursing through my veins!"

Lily smiled at her smugly. "And he's quite right, you know. I hadn't thought of it in just that way, but it seems to me to be true enough."

"I don't believe that either one of you knows me well enough to make such an observation, Lily."

Suddenly weary, Alexa sank back against the comfortable cushions of the coach and tried to close out Lily's chatter. She could not, however, forget Lily's parting shot that evening.

"He'll be here to see me as soon as it's decent to call tomorrow!" Lily said as she walked up the stairs beside Alexa. "I don't see how I shall be able to sleep a wink for the excitement of seeing him again!"

"And I'm certain that he feels just the same way," Alexa said, grateful she was opening her door and slipping inside to escape Lily.

"He does, you know!" Lily called after her. "You don't think he does, but he truly does! You'll see tomorrow!"

Alexa groaned to herself as she closed the door behind her. *Tomorrow!* She would have to play propriety in the drawing room with Lily and her callers, so she would once again be subjected to Lord Rivington's attentions. And how in heaven's name could she keep Lily from making a fool of herself—or from accepting him if he should decide to offer for her?

Why had she told Mrs. Lathrop that she would—or could—take care of her granddaughter? She thought of what a marriage between Lily and such a man as Rivington would be like and she winced. She could not allow it to happen. Even though Lily deserved a taking down, she did not deserve to make such an unhappy marriage—and after all, Alexa had promised Mrs. Lathrop that she would prevent just such a thing from occurring.

As she drifted off to sleep that night, Alexa thought of Rivington and seemed to hear him laughing at her. She punched her pillow vigorously and tried to close out the sound. He was quite an impossible man, and she had no patience with him.

* * *

We'd Like to Invite You to Subscribe to Zebra's Regency Romance Book Club and Give You a Gift of 4 Free Books as Your Introduction! (Worth $19.96!)

If you're a Regency lover, imagine the joy of getting 4 FREE Zebra Regency Romances and then the chance to have the lovely stories delivered to your home each month at the lowest prices available! Well, that's our offer to you and here's how you benefit by becoming a Zebra Home Subscription Service subscriber:

- **4 FREE** Introductory Regency Romances are delivered to your doors

- 4 BRAND NEW Regencies are then delivered each month (usually before they're available in bookstores)

- Subscribers save almost $4.00 every month

- Home delivery is always **FREE**

- You also receive a **FREE** monthly newsletter, *Zebra/ Pinnacle Romance News* which features author profiles, contests, subscriber benefits, book previews and more

- No risks or obligations...in other words you can cancel whenever you wish with no questions asked

Join the thousands of readers who enjoy the savings and convenience offered to Regency Romance subscribers. After your initial introductory shipment, you receive 4 brand-new Zebra Regency Romances each month to examine for 10 days. Then, if you decide to keep the books, you'll pay the preferred subscriber's price of just $4.00 per title. That's only $16.00 for all 4 books and there's never an extra charge for shipping and handling.

It's a no-lose proposition, so return the FREE BOOK CERTIFICATE today!

Say Yes to 4 Free Books!
Complete and return the order card to receive this $19.96 value, ABSOLUTELY FREE!

(If the certificate is missing below, write to:)
Zebra Home Subscription Service, Inc.,
120 Brighton Road, P.O. Box 5214, Clifton, New Jersey 07015-5214
or call TOLL-FREE 1-888-345-BOOK

FREE BOOK CERTIFICATE

YES! Please rush me 4 Zebra Regency Romances without cost or obligation. I understand that each month thereafter I will be able to preview 4 brand-new Regency Romances FREE for 10 days. Then, if I should decide to keep them, I will pay the money-saving preferred subscriber's price of just $16.00 for all 4...that's a savings of almost $4 off the publisher's price with no additional charge for shipping and handling. I may return any shipment within 10 days and owe nothing, and I may cancel this subscription at any time. My 4 FREE books will be mine to keep in any case.

Name _____

Address_____ Apt. _____

City_____ State_____ Zip _____

Telephone ( ) _____

Signature _____
(If under 18, parent or guardian must sign.)

RG0B99

Terms and prices subject to change. Orders subject to acceptance by Zebra Home Subscription Service, Inc.

The next day was fully as trying as Alexa had expected it to be. As they sat in the drawing room receiving guests, a number of bouquets were delivered to Lily from admirers, among them an armful of long-stalked creamy lilies.

"They're from Rivington, of course," Lily said triumphantly as she tossed down the card and glanced at Alexa. "He says that he is counting the minutes until he can see me again."

"I hope he doesn't strain his intellect doing so," Alexa murmured, not intending for anyone to hear her.

However, Philip Forest, who had arrived a few minutes earlier and received no more than a casual hello from Lily, caught Alexa's eye and smiled.

"I assure you that he has intellect to spare, Miss Howard," he said. There was no hint of reproach in his voice, but Alexa blushed.

"Forgive my poor manners, Mr. Forest. I did not intend for anyone to hear me. I must learn to guard my tongue. I am far too inclined to say what I think without consideration of the consequences."

"In other words, you are honest," Mr. Forest replied. "That is something to be proud of, rather than ashamed of."

Alexa laughed. "Thank you for putting such a positive face on my abominable lapse of manners, Mr. Forest. I promise that I shall do better."

"I think you do wonderfully well as it is," he returned. Then he added in a low voice, "I know myself how difficult your position in this household must be as companion to Miss Lathrop. I am not unfamiliar with such a position, as you know."

Alexa flushed, knowing that he too must think that she was a poor relative taken in by her family. It scarcely seemed kind to tell him that she was quite independent and that she was there only as a kindness to her guardian. As it was, he clearly considered her his confederate because of their similar positions in Society, and she appreciated his readiness to become her comrade. She was in need of friends.

Mistaking the reason for her flush, he patted her hand comfortingly. "Forgive me for making you uneasy, Miss Howard," he said gently. "It was just my clumsy way of telling you that I place myself at your disposal. Whenever I may be of service, please feel free to call upon me."

She smiled at him gratefully. "You are very kind, Mr. Forest. I hope that Lord Rivington doesn't mind your generous offer."

Philip shook his head. "As I told you, ma'am, you mistake the manner of man he is. He has told me that I am to help you in whatever way possible."

Alexa murmured her thanks again, glancing dubiously at Rivington, who, having arrived a short time before, had wasted no time in snaring Lily for himself. To her chagrin, he caught her eye and winked.

Lily noted the exchange and turned to frown at Alexa. "Well, really, Alexa, I should think that, even though your father was in trade, you would have better manners than to attempt a flirtation when I am talking with Rivington."

"I assure you, Lily, that I was not attempting to flirt

with Lord Rivington, nor am I interested in any such flirtation.'' Her tone was sharper than she intended, and Rivington's eyes gleamed.

''You show me no quarter, ma'am,'' he protested. ''At this rate, I shall soon have only shreds of my self-respect left. Surely you could consent to at least a light flirtation.''

Lily sniffed. ''Alexa has no notion how to go about an elegant flirtation,'' she announced. ''No one who has not been bred to such niceties can be expected to observe them. You shall have to rely upon me, Lord Rivington.''

He bent over her hand and smiled into her eyes. ''It will be my pleasure, Miss Lathrop,'' he assured her.

Alexa groaned inwardly. Lily's eyes were wide; she obviously believed every word he was telling her. Her vanity had always been indulged, and she had been reared to believe that there was no one more lovely or more desirable than she. Any simpleton could see as much and play upon her weakness, and Rivington was very far from being a simpleton.

Remembering Mrs. Lathrop's command to her, Alexa rose and walked to the window, staring at the garden in the center of the square. She had forgotten Mr. Forest, who very quickly joined her.

''Please don't let Rivington upset you, ma'am,'' he said in a low voice, glancing over his shoulder at the laughing pair across the room. ''He meant nothing by his careless words, I promise you.''

''It isn't Rivington who upsets me,'' said Alexa. ''Or

rather, it isn't what he says to me that is distressing. Just look at Lily. She is drinking in his every word."

Troubled, Mr. Forest followed her glance and nodded. "Miss Lathrop does appear to be impressed. That is quite normal for a young woman where Rivington is concerned, however."

Deciding that she had little to lose by being blunt with the young man, who had already expressed his friendship for her, Alexa came straight to the point.

"Forgive my directness, Mr. Forest, but I understand that Lord Rivington intends to marry an heiress such as Lily to ease his financial situation. I intend to see that Lily is not his choice. I have an obligation to her grandmother."

Mr. Forest stared at her, startled. "It's true enough that he has suffered some setbacks, but he is not, I believe, in the serious straits that you would indicate."

Alexa blushed. "I may be wrong," she admitted, "but I was told that, and I had no reason to doubt the speaker."

"You don't know London Society well, Miss Howard," said Mr. Forest consolingly, "so you would have no reason to disbelieve the person who told you as much. However, I must add that very frequently rumormongers have their own axes to grind."

Alexa nodded. "That could well be true," she admitted, "although I confess I wanted to believe that Lord Rivington is capable of doing such a thing."

Once again, he stared at her. "Why would you wish him to be such a blackguard?" he asked.

"Perhaps that would make him much less charming," she said thoughtfully. "I could give myself as many good reasons for avoiding him as I would the plague.''

Mr. Forest shook his head firmly. ''I would do anything to help you, ma'am,'' he said, ''but I am afraid that you have greatly mistaken Lord Rivington's character. You do him a grave injustice.''

''Perhaps,'' she shrugged. ''In the meantime, I think it safer that Miss Lathrop keep her distance from him.''

Mr. Forest nodded. ''Doubtless that's true,'' he agreed. ''Young girls are far too inclined to fall in love with him, and that does make his life difficult.''

''I can imagine that it must,'' Alexa agreed, ''and I have seen that Lord Rivington is not a man equipped to face difficulty. I will do all that I can to see that he need not face that particular difficulty where we are concerned.''

''And just what difficulty do you plan to spare me, Miss Howard?'' Lord Rivington inquired lazily.

Without Alexa or Forest taking note of it, he had risen from his place and quietly strolled up behind them.

''If I did not know Miss Howard's puritanical proclivities, I might suspect a flirtation,'' he observed, noting with amusement her quick flush and his secretary's startled expression.

''You take too much pleasure in discomfiting other people, sir,'' Alexa said shortly. ''I can only hope that the favor will soon be returned.''

''I feel certain that, given the opportunity, you will return it in spades, Miss Howard,'' he acknowledged gracefully, making her a slight bow. "And I will then have cause to be doubly grateful to you."

"Doubly grateful?" Alexa remarked suspiciously. "Just what do you mean by that, sir?"

"Only that it would of course be a pleasure to me to see you return the favor, as you so graciously phrased it. And as I understand from what you were saying to Mr. Forest, you are already endeavoring to spare me the necessity of facing some difficulty. Although I do not know what the particular difficulty is that you are planning to spare me, I am deeply grateful for your efforts. As you so aptly observed, I am not a man equipped to face difficulty."

"Whatever are the three of you gabbling about?" Lily demanded crossly. Unable to bear not being the center of attention any longer, she had left her chair and joined them at the window.

"Nothing of consequence," Alexa responded quickly, taking advantage of the interruption.

"I didn't think so. It sounded like so much taradiddle to me." Glancing at Lord Rivington, Lily smiled invitingly and took his arm, leading him back to his place across the room. "Do come back and entertain me with your stories, and leave these two to talk to one another."

Lord Rivington followed her, but Alexa had the satisfaction of seeing him glance several times at her and Mr. Forest as they continued their conversation. She was quite certain that he understood her disapproval and the reason for it. Perhaps he would think twice before attempting to engage Lily's affections. Then again, she reflected, he was a man who thought very highly of himself. Quite possibly he felt that she would be able to do little to halt his progress if she wished to do so. That thought made her more determined than ever to thwart him.

The next few days were a whirl of activity. Alexa and Lily attended breakfasts and evening parties, paid calls and shopped and received callers, rode in the park, visited the theater, and enjoyed their first real ball. It seemed to Alexa that everywhere she turned she encountered Lord Rivington, and his attentions to Lily were most pronounced.

To her displeasure, she found herself alone with him for a moment just two days later. She was the first one to enter the drawing room that afternoon, and he was the first caller shown in.

"What bad luck for you, Miss Howard," he said sympathetically, noting her expression as the butler showed him in and understanding it all too well.

Embarrassed by her lack of good breeding, Alexa immediately forced a smile and said, "Not at all, Lord Rivington. It is you, I fear, who has the lack of luck. I am certain that you had far rather have found Miss Lathrop here alone."

He looked at her speculatively. "Had you considered the possibility that your idea is very far from the truth?" he asked.

She looked at him in surprise. "Of course not," she replied. "You have made no secret of your interest in her, nor of your lack of interest in me."

Alexa noted uncomfortably that his eyes once again were filled with laughter, although his expression remained serious. She suspected that she was about to be roasted, and she had no notion of how best to protect herself. He seemed to enjoy sparring with her, and she was uncertain as to the rules of the game.

"Ah, but there you would be very wrong, Miss Howard. I am most interested in you."

"And why would that be, sir?" she inquired coolly, refusing to allow herself to be drawn. She was not sure of his object, but she was determined to deprive him of what pleasure she could.

"Why, for the pleasure of your company, of course," he returned smoothly, smiling at her blandly.

"You are not serious, sir. After all, I am merely, as you have noted, Miss Lathrop's companion."

"And a companion whose family has been in trade," he amended, his eyes gleaming. "I listen carefully, Miss Howard."

"I am not ashamed of the fact that my father was in trade, sir," she responded. "He committed a sin greater than that, however."

Lord Rivington looked interested. "Indeed?" he inquired curiously. "Have you skeletons hidden in your family closet, my little Puritan?"

"I am neither yours nor a Puritan, Lord Rivington," she returned, pausing to straighten some flowers in their vase on her way to the window overlooking the street. "His greater sin was that he lost all of his money. So, as you see, I am a companion to a lady whose family has never been in trade and whose family has wisely retained all of its funds."

"Very wise, indeed," he agreed, all laughter gone

from his eyes. "In truth, as you and I both know, Miss Howard, money is a necessary evil in this world."

It was all true, she thought. What she had heard was undoubtedly true. He had no money himself, and he would be obliged to marry for it. Lily was very far from safe, and Alexa's heart was curiously heavy when she thought it likely that Lord Rivington would attempt to marry Lily.

Before she could think of an appropriate way to respond, a new caller was announced, and the butler's disapproval was clear in every tone. To Alexa's amazed delight, it was Captain Derringer. The young man, although clearly aware that he was out of his element, was poised and calm, and Alexa was proud of him. She didn't need to blush for him in front of Lord Rivington.

After the introductions were made, there was an awkward pause. Lord Rivington was obviously interested in knowing about the captain and his relationship with Alexa, and it was clear that the captain did not wish to speak in front of him of private matters. To Alexa's relief, Lily swept into the room and Alexa was able to bear the captain away to the library for a private interview, well aware that Lord Rivington's gaze had followed them to the door.

"What a pleasant surprise, Captain Derringer," Alexa said, turning to take his hand when the entered the privacy of the library. "I had not thought to see you again until next winter."

"Nor I you, Miss Howard," he returned eagerly. "I had planned to spend this time with my mother, as I told you, but a most extraordinary opportunity came my way, and I am about to set sail once again. This time for Barbados.''

"Indeed?'' she asked, her interest sincere. "What is taking you there?''

"A new business venture, ma'am—one that I hope will benefit you as well as myself.''

"And what might that be, Captain Derringer? Are you going to bring back sugar from the plantations there?''

He nodded eagerly. "And one of those plantations, I believe, is the one that belonged to your father, Miss Howard.''

She stared at him a moment. "But that one burned to the ground, Captain Derringer—years ago.''

"Yes, I know that it did, but it has been long enough now for the new growth to come back again and for it once again to produce.''

"But wouldn't Mr. Lawrence know about it?'' she asked, puzzled. Her father's solicitor had been very faithful in looking after her small affairs for all the years since her parents' deaths.

"He will know now,'' said Captain Derringer. "I plan to see him later today. Only yesterday did I receive a letter from the broker I will be buying from, and he referred to the names of several of the plantations whose sugar he purchases. And I recognized your father's.''

Alexa sat quite still. If what Captain Derringer said were true, then her circumstances when she came of age in June would be more than merely comfortable. She would be an heiress. She sighed and put her face in her hands. If only her parents could have lived to see this. . . .

Distressed, Captain Derringer put out his hand and touched her shoulder lightly. "I didn't mean to cause you pain, Miss Howard," he said apologetically. "I only wanted to help to repay all your father did for me."

Alexa looked up and smiled a little tearfully. "That's quite all right, Captain. I'm crying because I'm happy, not because you've distressed me."

At that inappropriate moment, the door opened and Lord Rivington appeared.

"Why, Miss Howard," he said dryly, "I had no idea that you were subject to the more tender emotions. Pray forgive my intrusion." And he closed the door quietly.

The captain and Alexa both flushed uncomfortably. The man had a knack for saying and doing disconcerting things that disturbed one's peace of mind. He had no business at all coming to the library and intruding upon them. Maddening, annoying man!

"I hope that I haven't created a problem for you, Miss Howard," the captain said.

"Not at all," she returned quickly, extending her hand to him. "You have brought happy news, sir, and I greatly appreciate it. You have been very faithful."

He took her hand eagerly. "No more than your father was to me. I am glad that I have been able to help you at least a little."

"More than a little," she assured him, making arrangements to meet him in the park the next afternoon so that they could avoid the embarrassment of another misinterpreted visit.

Fortunately, the next day was a balmly one, and Alexa thoroughly enjoyed their stroll in the park. Her enjoyment was increased when they encountered Sophia Halleck, Lord Rivington's sister, who was walking with a friend.

"You are Robert's young friend, are you not?" Sophia inquired, smiling as they drew closer to one another.

Alexa, somewhat bemused by being referred to as Lord Rivington's "young friend," took a moment to respond, then nodded, and turned to introduce Captain Derringer.

A single glance told her that the captain was completely bewitched by the vision of femininity before him. Although never a talkative man, he could at first scarcely be cajoled into speaking a word, but once Sophia understood what he did, she turned upon him with a glowing face.

"The captain of a ship?" she asked. "How exciting that must be! How I have longed to travel the world and see the strange things that you doubtless have seen!"

Alexa, who had been fearful that introducing him would be awkward if Sophia considered him to far beneath her in social rank to take notice of, was relieved by her open interest in his work. Captain Derringer, as soon as he could recover his voice, began to answer her questions as thoroughly and patiently as he could.

"She is a lovely young woman, is she not?" Alexa

inquired innocently after Sophia and her friend had left them.

"Yes, she is," replied the captain flatly, his mind clearly miles away. They walked on a few minutes in silence; then he asked abruptly, "Is her husband a gentleman named Charles Halleck?"

"I don't know," she replied, caught off guard. She was aware that Sophia was married, but she knew little more than that. "Why do you ask?"

His face was grave. "I met the gentleman once," he replied. "It has been some time ago, though."

"You sound disapproving, Captain. Is there something amiss with Mr. Halleck?"

He nodded. "I don't like to gossip, Miss Howard, but I think that you should know."

"Know what?" she asked curiously.

"When I sailed for your parents the first time, there was another gentleman connected with my voyage."

"Mr. Halleck?" she inquired, trying to prod him a little.

Captain Derringer nodded. "He owned the ship I sailed, the *Maria*. He won it gambling one night just before we left Liverpool."

"Does he own the ship still?"

He shook his head. "He didn't even manage to hang on to it until we left harbor. He had already lost it to someone else. And I understand that he has continued to gamble. Thinking that I'd be interested in the man that once owned my ship, one of my bankers told me that Halleck has also finally managed to gamble away his entire estate."

Alexa stared at him. "He lost his estate?"

Captain Derringer nodded again.

"His poor wife must be beside herself," she said slowly. "Mrs. Halleck seemed quite herself, however."

Captain Derringer shrugged. "Perhaps since he has always been a gambler, she has learned to live with it."

Alexa shook her head in disbelief. "However would one learn to live with something like that?"

The matter continued to trouble her. She liked Sophia Halleck, and it seemed terribly unfair that her life should be darkened by a husband with a penchant for gambling. Surely Lord Rivington was capable of taking the matter in hand, she thought. Or at least if anyone were capable of being high-handed enough to do so, he would be. With that hope, she was forced to be satisfied.

It was two days later, on the afternoon before their first ball, that Alexa realized that things were moving even faster in the relationship between Lord Rivington and Lily than she had realized.

To Alexa's surprise, a maid came to her chamber to inform her that she had a caller waiting in the drawing room. Since all of the callers thus far except for Captain Derringer had been for Lily, Alexa went downstairs quickly, half fearful that she would find the bearer of bad tidings below. The captain, she knew, was in Liverpool, making the final arrangements for his voyage.

And in some measure, the bearer of bad news was exactly whom she found. Mr. Forest rose as she entered the room and apologized profusely for intruding when he knew she would be busy preparing for the masquerade ball that evening.

"Nonsense, Mr. Forest," she replied briskly. "I have known for some time what my costume will be, so I am the mistress of my own time at the moment. Is there something in particular you wish to speak with me about?"

Recalled to the reason for his visit, Mr. Forest set his expression in sterner lines than Alexa had previously seen it, and he leaned toward her, speaking in a low voice.

"I am afraid, Miss Howard, that your fears about Lord Rivington are more accurate than I thought."

Alexa smiled grimly. "I was certain of that. But what has made you change your opinion, Mr. Forest? Has something happened?"

He nodded. "Two things have come to my attention that lead me to believe that Miss Lathrop might be about to elope with him."

Alexa sat up straighter, her eyebrows lifted. "To elope? So soon in their relationship?" she demanded. "I had not thought Lord Rivington could work quite so quickly."

"It appears that we both underestimated him," he replied reluctantly. "And it grieves me to say so."

"Yes, I can appreciate your loyalty to your employer," Alexa said impatiently, "but there is a young girl's future to be thought of, too."

"It is for that reason that I am here, Miss Howard," Mr. Forest said heavily. "As I told you, two things have come to my attention. First of all—" Here he paused, as though searching for the proper words.

"Yes, first of all?" Alexa prompted him.

"When opening his mail, which is one of my duties as his secretary, I inadvertently opened a letter that was intended for his eyes alone."

"A letter from Miss Lathrop?" she demanded.

He shook his head. "A letter from his solicitor reminding Lord Rivington of financial obligations it is imperative that he meet and suggesting that he sell some of his land."

Mr. Forest paused to stare at Alexa. "I don't know, Miss Howard, whether or not you realize it, but Lord Rivington would cut off his right hand before he would sell any of his property. Even though it is not entailed, he considers it his obligation to pass it on to his heir intact."

"A very noble sentiment," Alexa returned dryly. "And so he must suddenly acquire a very large amount of cash in order to keep his holdings?"

Mr. Forest nodded reluctantly, clearly unhappy to be divulging his employer's private affairs.

"And what is the second piece of news you have for me?" she asked. "Does it concern Miss Lathrop?"

Once again Forest nodded, his eyes on the toes of his boots. "He has acquired a special license from the Archbishop of Canterbury, and his valet is packing his bags for a two-week trip. He will leave directly after the masquerade tonight."

He looked at her and spoke abruptly. "And so you see, Miss Howard, that I felt I had no choice but to confide this to you. I had thought you very wrong in your estimate of Lord Rivington—and while I still think that you do not appreciate his good qualities, I could see that I had no choice but to tell you this so that we may take steps to protect Miss Lathrop.''

"We?" Alexa repeated, startled.

Forest nodded firmly. "His attentions to her have been most marked, and my conscience will not allow me to do other than to help you stop this elopement. If they wish to be married, then it must be with the proper permission from her family.''

Alexa did not trouble herself to tell him that Lily's father and stepmother would instantly give the marriage their blessing. Instead, she thought of Mrs. Lathrop.

"Well, we have a limited amount of time to lay our plans, Mr. Forest. You have had some time to consider matters. Do you have a suggestion?"

He shook his head apologetically. "Beyond seeing to it that Miss Lathrop does not enter his carriage, I'm afraid I have no particular plan. I was hoping that you, who know Miss Lathrop, would have an idea.''

Alexa thought swiftly. Lily planned to dress as Marie Antoinette that night, her dark hair covered by a towering white wig, a narrow red band of ribbon about her throat. Her face would be covered by a half mask. It would be easy enough to take her place. All that they really needed to know was how Lord Rivington planned to dress and where they were to meet.

Leaning close to Mr. Forest, she said in a low voice, "Now here is what we must do. . . .''

* * *

Alexa glanced about the ballroom, an unfamiliarly coquettish smile fixed on her lips. The mask irritated her, for it obscured her vision, and the wig made her feel as if she were wearing a large pineapple on the top of her head. Added to that were the cumbersome weight of the heavy, panniered gown and the tottering insecurity of high-heeled red slippers. She thought longingly for a moment of her own flat-heeled slippers and the slim, light gowns that allowed a woman freedom of movement. Women of thirty years earlier had had entirely too much to contend with, she decided. Contemporary fashions were much more to her taste.

Alexa thought of Lily sleeping peacefully upstairs and smiled in satisfaction. A few minutes ago she had informed the girl that her costume needed some adjustment and, having gotten her upstairs to a private chamber, had set down her own glass of wine while she knelt to make the imaginary repair.

"Be certain that you don't drink any of my wine, Lily," she had said in a voice of firm authority, still kneeling behind her. "You are much too young and it will make your head swim."

The warning had precisely the effect she had hoped for, and Lily had drained the glass in one long swallow. The wine alone would more than likely have been enough to make Lily sleepy, but Alexa had added a dose of laudanum to be certain that it would work quickly.

"You may be right, Alexa," Lily said thickly, beginning to sway. "I don't believe that I feel at all well. . . ."

Alexa had eased Lily onto a bed and managed to remove her gown and wig, laying out her own simple shepherdess costume on a nearby chair. She quickly dressed herself in Lily's outfit, then carefully placed a coverlet over the sleeping girl.

Stepping to the bellpull, she rang for a maid. When the woman entered the room, Alexa indicated the sleeping girl and said, "This is Miss Lathrop. She was taken ill and needs to rest. If she doesn't awaken before the ball is over, summon her parents from the party." She slipped a guinea in the woman's hand to ensure her aid and left the room, rejoining the throng in the ballroom.

Now all she needed to do was to locate Lord Rivington. Suddenly, she felt an arm firmly about her waist and a deep voice whispered, "Ah, *chérie*, what a vision you are. No real man could have allowed you to go to the guillotine."

Startled, Alexa glanced up into Lord Rivington's dark eyes before she could catch herself; then she glanced quickly down and fluttered her fan between them and smiled coquettishly, carefully avoiding saying anything—or meeting his eyes again. She had no desire for Lord Rivington to discover yet that he had been duped.

"You're very quiet tonight, Lily," he observed. "Surely you aren't having second thoughts about our plan."

Alexa plied her fan more energetically and shook

her head in denial, managing a fair imitation of Lily's shrill giggle.

"I am relieved to hear it," he said in a low voice.

Alexa could hear the smug satisfaction in his voice and she longed to rap him with the fan. Fortunately, however, she managed to fight the impulse.

"Are you ready?" he asked, his voice still low—and far too intimate, she thought grimly.

Alexa nodded.

"Then I will be waiting for you at the corner in my carriage. Use the side door I showed you so that you avoid the carriages lined up in front of the house."

Alexa nodded and Lord Rivington melted into the crowd. She would indeed meet him in the carriage, she thought, but it would scarcely be the lovers' reunion that he hoped for.

In less than a quarter of an hour, she joined him, a dark domino shrouding her, and she sank down upon the seat facing him. At a sign from him, the carriage moved briskly down the street.

"Why so distant, love?" he asked curiously, patting the cushion beside him. "Are you already angry with me?"

Alexa shook her head coyly, hoping to continue the charade for as long as she could. There was little chance that he could return to the ball and revive Lily, but she wouldn't put it past him to try to do so. The farther away they got from his intended bride, the better. And, she hoped, Mr. Forest would not be far behind them. He had sworn that he would not let the carriage out of his sight.

"No? Then are you being coy? You surprise me,

Lily dear. You assured me that you are no ice queen like your Miss Howard. I had thought you would be anxious to prove to me the truth of your statement.''

Alexa shook her head violently. Lord Rivington studied her for a moment, then sighed and leaned back against the cushions. "Very well then, ma'am. Enjoy your solitude—at least until we reach Kentland. Far be it from me to press my attentions upon a young lady who does not wish them—even if the young lady is about to become my wife.''

Alexa's eyes flew to his face. Kentland! So he thought he was taking Lily to his home to be married! Mr. Forest had told her that might be the case. Well, she told herself, there would be no need to make the entire journey. Another hour or so would put them far enough away from Lily that he could not try to accomplish his purpose that night. Resolutely, she closed her eyes and pretended to sleep.

Rivington made no attempt to disturb her, and the time seemed to move by very slowly. Finally, Alexa decided that enough time had passed, and she sat up abruptly, weary of the charade, the costume, and Lord Rivington.

"I believe, sir, that you may command your coachman to turn around and head back to London,'' she announced briskly, holding herself very straight in preparation for his reaction.

For a moment, he stared at her, his eyes wide. It was a bright night and moonlight washed her side of the coach. She had expected anger, but a slow smile lit his face.

"Well, who would ever have thought that a little

Puritan would have such a taste for romance?" he exclaimed, reaching out and pulling her next to him, managing the difficulties presented by her panniered gown with amazing dexterity. One arm kept her firmly in place.

"Miss Howard, I must admit that I am shocked— but a little pleased—to have you show such a determined interest in me." His voice held the mockery that had become so familiar to her, and his free hand caressed her cheek in a most disconcerting manner.

"You know very well that I have no interest at all in you, Lord Rivington—save what I must have to keep Lily out of trouble!" she replied indignantly, trying to ignore her helpless circumstances and his wandering hand. "And I am neither a Puritan nor a Methodist—not that it is any of your business, sir!"

"It seems to be very much my business, Miss Howard," he pointed out affably. "After all, it is you who have chosen to join me in my solitary trip to my home. That would seem to me to indicate a strong interest in me—and not an entirely ladylike interest, wouldn't you say?" To her dismay, he leaned closer and his lips brushed her cheek, then her chin.

"If you would stop being so perverse, sir, perhaps you could bring yourself to turn this carriage around and start back to London!" she said sharply.

Lord Rivington settled himself more comfortably on the seat, still keeping her firmly beside him, and propped his boots on the seat across from them.

"Why, Miss Howard, I would not deprive you of the trip to Kentland that you seem so eager to make. It would be quite unchivalrous of me. Do make yourself comfortable, for we have an hour or more to go, and I plan to be—what was your word for it?—perverse for the rest of the time."

"You don't know the meaning of the word *chivalrous*," she replied bitterly, painfully aware that for the moment he had—quite literally—the upper hand.

"You wrong me, Miss Howard," he said reproachfully, his finger tracing the line of her cheek. "I was quite a fair student in my time, you know, and I still occasionally read a book or two. Not often, of course," he assured her, "just often enough to remain literate."

Alexa decided to change her attack. "You might as well take me back, sir. You don't wish to marry me, and Lily will be very cross when she discovers what you've done."

She could see the flash of white that was his smile. "I should think that *cross* will sadly understate her mood, Miss Howard. My heart almost goes out to you when I think of what she will say to you when she learns that you have deprived her of her elopement with a lord. She has the temperament of a fishwife, you know."

Alexa stared at him in astonishment. Men usually saw no more than Lily's very pleasing facade. "You realize that?" she asked blankly.

"Of course, I realize that. I do wish, Miss Howard," he said plaintively, "that you would stop acting as though I am not playing with a full deck. I'm not accustomed to being thought deficient—at least in intelligence."

"If you realize Lily's temperament, then you are

quicker than most of your sex," she said frankly. She was silent a moment, then added, "And if you knew, I cannot imagine why you would wish to marry her."

He smiled, and once again she could see the flash of white. "There are times, dear Miss Howard, when we must do things for a greater good."

"How noble you sound!" Alexa exclaimed acidly. She had almost come to enjoy this aggravating man, yet he was showing her all too clearly that he had neither scruples nor reservations about what he would do to sustain his way of life.

"Yes, don't I?" he responded wryly, clearly laughing at himself. "I have almost convinced myself."

That was possibly the most annoying thing about him, Alexa thought to herself. He was by far the most disarming man she had ever met. He would say something outrageous, and then throw her completely off balance by following it with something amusing or tender or self-deprecating. She reminded herself sternly that Mrs. Lathrop had entrusted Lily's welfare to her, and this man had not thought twice about eloping with her—when he clearly had no particular use for Lily as a person.

"But not completely?" she inquired. "You don't believe yourself?"

Rivington shook his head, chuckling. "How could I believe what I say when I have my good little conscience traveling with me?" he asked. "Were I to forget myself, you would call me to order in no time at all. I have every confidence in your ability to point out my shortcomings, Miss Howard."

"If you mean what you say, sir, then I demand that

you set me free. I am most uncomfortable being held like this."

"I would not wish for you to be uncomfortable, Miss Howard," he replied in a low voice. "But since you make me so uncomfortable, dear lady, it seems only fair that I return at least a portion of the favor."

And he swept her into his arms and kissed her so firmly that she no longer remembered to breathe. When she did, she could scarcely gasp for breath, and her Marie Antoinette wig fell off, tumbling to a heap in the floor of the carriage.

"Well, really, Lord Rivington!" she said indignantly, determined to mask her reaction to his kiss. "Your behavior is completely outrageous! It should be your wedding night and yet you are pressing your attentions upon another young woman!"

Alexa could see his shoulders shaking and knew, in a wave of intense irritation, that he was laughing at her again.

"As you say, Miss Howard, this *should* be my wedding night. That it is not is strictly because of your interference, so don't you feel a trifle hypocritical when you criticize my behavior—especially since you have placed yourself in my company in, shall we say, very intimate circumstances?"

"I do not!" she assured him. "I am merely fulfilling my obligation to Lily's grandmother!"

"Ah, Lily's grandmother," he mused. "I don't believe I have met the lady. Her father, yes—and her very attractive stepmother, who appears not to have much more wit than Lily—but I have not met the grandmother."

"Well, it stands to reason that you have not," Alexa snapped. "Her grandmother is an invalid and cannot come to London herself."

She could feel him studying her, his arm still firmly around her. She hoped that he could not see her as well as she could see him. That abominable wig was still lying on the floor, and she found herself wishing that she could at least pat her own hair into place. She was suddenly painfully aware that she must look quite terrible now that the wig had gone—not, of course, that it mattered at all what Rivington thought of her or her appearance.

"And so you are here as the grandmother's delegate," he mused. "And your duty is—"

"My duty is to see to it that Lily does not make an unhappy or an unsuitable marriage," she said stiffly, looking straight ahead instead of at him.

"And you feel that my marriage to Lily would be . . ." He paused, waiting for her to finish the thought.

"Would be both unhappy and unsuitable," she said, curiously reluctant to say that aloud. He deserved it, of course, but it still did sound both tasteless and cruel to give voice to the thought.

"I see," he said thoughtfully, his grip on her easing slightly as he turned to stare out the window of the coach. "I am certain that you are right, of course. Still . . ."

"Still what?" she inquired curiously.

He turned to her and smiled, his tone switching back to the familiar mocking one. "Still, Miss Howard, you must understand that it is very necessary that I make an advantageous marriage. I fear that Lily still offers that promise—even if she offers so little else.''

"You have no conscience at all," Alexa said bitterly, sinking back against the seat. He would doubtless continue to pursue Lily, who required no pursuit whatsoever. Alexa could not stay with the girl night and day, and Rivington was a clever man. She would not be able to trick him again.

"None," he agreed cheerfully. "I gave my conscience up when I was still quite young—it makes you so uncomfortable, you know—and I am greatly in favor of comfort.''

"Yes, I'm certain that you are," she replied grimly. "I doubt that you ever think of anything else other than your own creature comforts.''

"You wrong me yet again, Miss Howard," he exclaimed reproachfully. "As a matter of fact, I think quite often of you.''

"Of me?" she asked, startled. "Why would you think of me? Are you thinking of how you will next render my life uncomfortable?''

"Not at all," he chuckled. "I often find myself thinking that meeting you again will offer me great pleasure, and I assure you that there are very few things that give me pleasure these days.''

"I suppose that you mean that to be a compliment," she sniffed, secretly pleased that so critical a man should find her enjoyable. "If what you say is true, I should think that you would turn this carriage around immediately and return me to London.''

"And just why would I do that?" he demanded, his astonishment clear.

"You just said, sir, that meeting me gives you pleasure. If that is so—"

"*Since* that is so, I naturally would like to spend more time with you, Miss Howard. We may return to London tomorrow. Tonight, we are almost to Kentland, and tonight and tomorrow, I shall enjoy the pleasure of your company."

"I might have known that you would think only of yourself, Lord Rivington!" Alexa exclaimed, angry at his carelessness with her reputation. "You know that I would be ruined if I stayed with you tonight! Since you will not play the part of a gentleman, it is certainly just as well that I asked Mr. Forest to follow us."

"The devil you did!" he exclaimed. "You're having me followed by my own secretary?"

Alexa nodded, furious to feel a traitorous tear slipping down her cheek at her distress over his lack of regard for her. She did not believe in giving way to tears, and he would doubtless think her guilty of trying to use every feminine wile she could think of. All that she really wanted to do, she told herself, was to slap him. She could not help but feel, however, that slapping Rivington would not be wise.

"And why would he do such a thing, Miss Howard?" he demanded, his voice cold.

"Because he has more regard for me than do you, Lord Rivington," she replied, attempting to sound equally cold and distant. "He is interested in protecting both Lily and me—while you seem set upon bringing ruin upon us both."

"You have a taste for melodrama, Miss Howard," he observed coolly. "I would not have thought it."

"And you have a taste for playing the villain of the piece," she returned sharply. "And I *would* have thought that!"

Unexpectedly, his shoulders shook again. "You never disappoint me, my dear." He was quiet for a moment, his arm still firmly about her shoulder as he stared out the window thoughtfully. "I suppose that I should be grateful that you have not set the Bow Street Runners upon me."

"I hadn't thought of doing so," she replied simply, regret in her voice, and again she felt his shoulders shake.

"I didn't think that you would tell me that I did *not* deserve the Turkish treatment I would receive from those officers of the law," he observed lightly.

"You!" she exclaimed. "It is not you who have received Turkish treatment, but *I!* I have been thrown about like so much luggage, abused to my face, and—"

"And kissed," he added calmly.

"And kissed—although it was done by force," she added indignantly, her jaws tight. "You have not treated me as a lady, but as a strumpet!"

Rivington's laughter rang through the coach while Alexa maintained what she hoped was a dignified and frozen silence.

Finally regaining his composure, he took a handkerchief from his pocket so that he could wipe his eyes. "Miss Howard, I can think of no one less like a strumpet than you."

"But I—" she began, but he held up his free hand remonstratingly.

"Nor have you the slightest notion of how a strumpet would be treated, ma'am. I assure you I have not done what you have accused me of doing."

Her cheeks hot, she attempted to maintain her dignity by retiring into silence. He watched her for a moment, then released his hold on her and leaned out the window to shout at his coachman.

Having been assured that the coach would be turned back toward London at the first opportunity offered by the road, Rivington settled back into his place and placed his arm about Alexa once more, patting her shoulder in what she considered a most patronizing manner.

"Now, you see, Miss Howard, you may rest more easily. We will soon be driving in the direction you have so earnestly requested."

"We must watch for Mr. Forest," she said anxiously. "I do hope that he has stayed close to us. It could be quite dangerous for a horseman alone."

"It could be quite dangerous for Mr. Forest if he comes *too* close to me this evening," Rivington observed grimly. "I'm afraid that I take a very dim view of having my affairs interfered with by my servants."

Alarmed by his serious tone of voice, Alexa hurried into speech. "Oh, you mustn't blame Mr. Forest, sir. It is all my fault—you must believe me. Pray don't be angry with him."

"I have no trouble believing that you are behind all of this, ma'am, but I still cannot have my own secretary plotting against me."

"Not plotting," she remonstrated. "At least not really plotting. Mr. Forest thinks very highly of you,

Lord Rivington, and he was *most* reluctant to lend me his support."

"But you convinced him?" Rivington queried.

Alexa nodded, made miserable by her sudden realization that she might have cost Mr. Forest the job that he needed so badly.

"Pray don't hold him responsible, Lord Rivington. I am the one who is at fault, you know. He was only trying to do the gentlemanly thing."

"Ah," said Rivington, "a chivalrous gentleman—unlike myself."

"Don't put words in my mouth!" Alexa protested. "I wasn't trying to compare the two of you."

"But you did so," he observed dryly, "and I see that I did not fare well in the process."

He paused a moment, and she remained silent, afraid of making him more angry. "I suppose I should be grateful that you did not call in your young captain tonight, too. He probably would have set upon me with a pistol."

"Captain Derringer?" she asked, startled. "Why would I have him follow you?"

"He is very interested in you and your welfare, is he not?" inquired Rivington. "Or at least that is the way it appeared to me when I saw the two of you together in the library—and then later in the park. Very cozy, it seemed to me."

"He has been a good friend," she replied stiffly. "I'm sure that I don't know what you mean by cozy. That is merely some figment of your own distorted imagination."

He made her a brief bow. "Thank you for your vote of confidence, ma'am."

They came suddenly to a halt. The coach, having turned about and headed once more toward London, had indeed encountered Mr. Forest. Following Rivington's instructions, he tethered his mount to the carriage and climbed in to sit with them.

"And so, Philip, I understand that you have been making my private affairs *your* private affairs," Rivington observed in an affable tone.

"I beg your pardon for any distress I have caused you, sir," Mr. Forest replied, his voice strained, "but I did not feel that my conscience would allow—"

Rivington held up his hand. "Please, Philip, do show me a little mercy. It has been an extraordinarily long day, and I refuse to allow you to unburden yourself of your conscience at this ungodly hour. I must sleep."

And accordingly, he leaned back against the seat and closed his eyes, soon breathing easily and sinking into a peaceful slumber.

Mr. Forest and Alexa, after looking blankly at one another for a moment, smiled—a little bleakly—and soon allowed themselves to sink into sleep as well.

It was as well that Alexa rested on the return journey, for there was little rest when she arrived at the Lathrop home in London. The lights were ablaze and the family had just recently returned home without her.

"How shameless!" Mrs. Lathrop exclaimed, meeting her at the front door.

Lord Rivington and Mr. Forest stood on either side of her, and it was Rivington who bowed and spoke. "I'm afraid that there has been a misunderstanding," he began, but Mrs. Lathrop cut him off.

"Indeed there has been!" she said sharply. "And it was my mother-in-law who made it. I cannot imagine why she sent such an underbred and dangerous young woman as a companion for Lily! Imagine her drugging a girl like Lily! We most certainly cannot allow a young and innocent girl to be exposed to such cruel and wanton behavior."

Alexa was prepared for Rivington to glance at her in amusement, but his eyes were cold as he looked at Mrs. Lathrop with distaste.

"As I said, madam, there has been a mistake. I had thought that I had been joined in the carriage by your stepdaughter. Since Miss Howard was wearing your stepdaughter's costume, and since she went to sleep almost as soon as she entered the carriage, it was some time later before I realized my mistake."

The Lathrops looked at him blankly. "What are you talking about?" Mr. Lathrop demanded finally. "My daughter most certainly would not have had a secret assignation with a man."

"I'm afraid that perhaps you do not know your daughter as well as you think you do," Rivington said gently.

Lathrop's face turned a distressing shade of purple, and for a moment, Alexa feared that he would have an attack of apoplexy.

"By God, I'll call you out, sir, if you say such a thing about my daughter again!"

"Then I'm afraid that you will have to do so," Rivington returned calmly. "But dueling is no longer considered acceptable, I'm afraid, and I must warn you that I am an admirable shot and a formidable swordsman. I beg you to reconsider."

"Is Lily feeling better?" Alexa asked anxiously, hoping to divert attention from the matter at hand.

"No thanks to you," Lily's stepmother returned crisply. "She had a terrible headache and went straight to bed when we got her home. She was most distraught."

"I have quite the headache myself," said Alexa. "I believe that I will go to bed, too. Pray excuse me, gentlemen."

The gentlemen bowed briefly, and Alexa made her way quickly up the stairs, careful not to catch anyone's eye as she passed them. All she wanted was a good night's rest.

Her rest, unfortunately was all too short. Lily awakened Alexa at a most ungodly hour the next morning, barging into her chamber without knocking and pulling back the covers abruptly.

"I don't see how you can look any decent person in the face!" Lily announced, staring down at Alexa, who was trying to bring her eyes into focus.

"I don't believe I can," moaned Alexa. "I can't even open my eyes properly."

"How could you interfere with my elopement?"

Lily hissed. "I know what you did! You dressed up like me and took my place in the carriage! I wish that Rivington had made you walk back to London when he found out it was you! I hope that you're satisfied with what you've done!"

Sighing, Alexa reminded herself of Lily's grandmother and forced herself to speak in a reasonable voice. "No, Lily, I'm not," she said, sitting up in bed and looking the girl in the eye.

Somewhat taken aback, Lily said uncertainly, "Well, at least you regret what you've done."

"That's not what I said, Lily. I said that I'm not satisfied with what I've done."

Puzzled, the girl stared at her, and Alexa continued patiently. "I won't be satisfied until I'm certain that you're not going to elope with Lord Rivington and ruin your chances for happiness."

Lily snatched up a small china box and flung it at Alexa, who ducked just in time. It smashed against the wall, its pieces scattering across the covers of the bed.

"You're jealous!" Lily screamed. "That's all it is! You think that he ought to be interested in you, but he's not! It's me that he wants!"

"It's your money that he wants," Alexa returned calmly, picking up the shards of china and stacking them on the bedside table. "And I can see that you're quite willing to give it to him."

The door opened and Mr. Lathrop spoke sharply. "What is all of the noise about? You sound like a pair of fishwives!"

Alexa, thinking of Rivington's unflattering remark

about Lily, was hard pressed not to smile, but Lily, still furious, was forced into silence. She was far less certain than Alexa of what her father's attitude toward her attempted elopement might be.

Alexa, not anxious to encounter any member of the Lathrop family, dressed hurriedly and left the house. She had hoped to call upon Mr. Lawrence to see if he knew anything more about the business in Barbados, and it seemed to her that there could be no more propitious time than the present. In fact, it seemed a very good time to begin looking for the house she would take on her twenty-first birthday. With that in mind, she walked briskly along the street, her thoughts happily engaged.

"You look very well this morning, ma'am," an all too familiar voice said. Looking up, Alexa saw that Lord Rivington had pulled up next to her in his curricle. "Would you join me for a ride through the park, Miss Howard?" he inquired genially.

She stared at him for a moment. "I believe that I have spent quite enough time riding with you, sir!" she snapped and began once again to walk briskly down the street.

To her dismay, he kept pace with her, driving carefully alongside her and devoting his attention to her in a nonstop conversation that drew the amusement of passersby.

"If you had any decency, sir, you would drive on!" she hissed, her face growing pinker by the minute.

"I suppose I would, Miss Howard," he agreed amicably, "but then, as you have so frequently pointed out, I have no decency at all. Actually," he added thoughtfully, "it is a great relief not to have any, for then, you know, I need feel no obligation to adhere to any standards save my own. In fact—"

"Very well," she said, stepping to the curb and glaring at him. "If you are determined to continue talking to me—even though I am not responding— I will ride with you so that I will be spared the embarrassment of having every dandy along the street laughing at me."

"Oh, I don't believe they were laughing at you," Rivington said comfortingly, helping her into the curricle beside him. "I'm quite sure that they were just sharing your enjoyment of an unusual situation."

"I wasn't enjoying it," she informed him, "as you very well know. I am sure that I don't know just why you are determined to be a thorn in my side, Lord Rivington, but you are doing a singularly fine job of it."

"Curious," he mused. "I had found myself thinking precisely the same thing about you."

"Yes, well, we've been through that, haven't we? I have an obligation—"

"Yes, yes, I know—an obligation to Miss Lathrop's grandmother. I remember. And you made it abundantly clear that you have no wish to see me marry Miss Lathrop. But what I would like to know, Miss Howard, is just how you would suggest that I mend the state of my rather ragged fortune if I don't marry an heiress. My only other prospect is an extremely wealthy great-aunt who lives somewhere in Switzerland, and she is showing every sign of living past the century mark. I am not a magician, and the money must come from somewhere."

"Why not invest what capital you have cleverly?" Alexa asked him tartly. "Why not look about you and use your wits instead of expecting the money to fall into your lap?"

"And just where do you suggest that I look about?" he demanded.

"Captain Derringer is an enterprising man," she informed him. "You could do no better than to invest in his voyage to Barbados if it is still possible to do so. I've given Mr. Forest the same advice and I have invested my own money."

"Have you indeed?" he inquired in amusement. "Your pin money, I suppose."

"A little more than that," she assured him, unable to resist telling him the truth. "Although it is true that I have been the companion of Miss Lathrop's grandmother—and now of Miss Lathrop—I am not the penniless girl you have taken me for."

"Indeed?" he asked, fixing her with a speculative gaze. "Are you telling me that you are wealthy, Miss Howard?"

She nodded, smiling. "And you needn't think that you will be able to marry me, Lord Rivington, so please spare me any languid glances. I have no desire to marry you, sir, or anyone else I have met."

"Not even your captain?" he asked.

Alexa shook her head.

"Not even Philip?" Rivington demanded. "You seem terribly concerned about his welfare."

Alexa smiled again. "Perhaps he comes closest,"

she admitted, enjoying the fleeting expression of chagrin on Rivington's face at her words.

"Ah, well," he sighed, "I shall try to make myself more acceptable to you, Miss Howard, now that I know that you are a woman of means."

"It will do you no good at all, sir," she assured him.

"Probably not in terms of convincing you to marry me," he acknowledged, smiling, "but perhaps, now and then, you will allow me the pleasure of your company."

She allowed herself a brief smile. "Perhaps," she responded.

And over the next few weeks, she was distressed to discover how very much she enjoyed his company. It was a discovery that she had no intention of sharing with him. Indeed, she had a difficult enough time simply acknowledging as much to herself. He was everything that she cared for least: an intelligent man, wasteful of his own resources, both financial and personal—a man careless of the feelings of others.

Nonetheless, he was charming. He never denied his faults, nor did he try to disguise them. He simply was what he was.

At first, she fully expected him to try again to elope with Lily. Most certainly the girl was willing, and for days, Alexa tried to be her shadow. Finally, however, she relaxed her watch. If Lord Rivington planned on keeping Lily's interest, he was going about it in a strange way. He kept his distance from Lily, and Lily promptly gave her attention to the other men who swarmed about her.

When they encountered Rivington now and then at parties, he was studiously polite to Lily and comfortably annoying to Alexa. Alexa had made it her business to note the wealthy young women and to share that information with him, never missing an opportunity to point him in the direction of a marital prospect that would suit his financial needs.

At a ball some two months after the attempted elopement, he surprised her by strolling over to her and speaking to her affably.

"And so, Miss Howard, tomorrow you will be twenty-one years of age, and you will come into your inheritance. What do you propose to do to celebrate the occasion?"

"I am taking a house here in London," she replied, watching him warily.

"Indeed?" he mused thoughtfully. "Might I be permitted to see it, perhaps even to accompany you there?"

"And why would you wish to do so, Lord Rivington?" she asked bluntly.

He raised one dark eyebrow. "Why, for the pleasure of your company, of course," he responded.

Alexa was far from certain that such was the case, but she finally agreed that he could visit the house with her the next day. She knew that he had something on his mind, but just what that was, she could not decide.

The next afternoon, he strolled after her into the charming rose garden behind her new house.

"Delightful!" he said sincerely, gazing about him. "An excellent choice, Miss Howard—not that I believe you could make any other kind of choice."

"I'm pleased that you like it, sir," she responded, looking about her happily.

As she was admiring her new estate, she was suddenly sharply aware that he was standing far too close to her, and she attempted to take a step back.

Catching her in his arms, he pressed her close, smiling at her discomfiture. "And now, my dear Miss Howard, on this, your twenty-first birthday, will you consent to be my wife?"

"You must think that I'm not in full possession of my faculties, sir!" she replied indignantly, trying to remove herself from his very firm grip. "How great a simpleton do you take me for? I know very well that you have in mind marrying my money—not me!"

"Ah, but there you would be wrong, my dearest shrew," he sighed. "I have no need of your money. We will have a solicitor attend to it so that it is entirely your own and I may not touch it."

She stared at him a moment. "How will you manage then?" she asked suspiciously. "I would not support your households, sir, even if I could. You are far too great a wastrel."

He shook his head in woeful agreement. "I suspect that I shall have to entrust myself to you, dear Alexa— although I am certain that I shall regret it and shall live the rest of my life under the cat's paw."

Seeing that she was still waiting for more solid information, he sighed again. "I fear that Great-Aunt Elmira in Switzerland has left me a very wealthy man, and

I am certain that your Captain Derringer will do his own small part in returning my investment several times over."

"You invested your money with him after all?" she demanded in amazement, for he had annoyed her greatly by insisting that he had made no such investment.

"How could I let you know that you rule me in such a manner?" he inquired sweetly. "You are already impossible. Why should I encourage you?"

"To show me that you take me seriously!" she replied sharply. "I know that you have taken me as a joke all along."

Rivington shook his head. "And now you know that you have been wrong, my dear. And what intense satisfaction it gives me to be able to say that to you," he added, smiling gently. "Will you consent now to marry me and let me share this house with you? After all, you can see that I have no need of your money."

"And what about your gambling?" she asked and was startled to see his sharp glance at her.

"And what makes you think that I am a gambler?" he demanded.

Caught off guard, she hesitated for a moment. "Gossip," she replied humbly. "Isn't it true?"

"To a degree," he admitted, "but not to the extent that people would have you believe." He mused for a moment, staring at one of the roses. Then he added slowly, "And this is not my own to tell, and I would not if I were speaking to anyone save you, my dear, but the gambling is a problem for another member of my family, not for me."

Alexa stared at him. "Sophia's husband?" she asked.

He looked at her in surprise. "Yes. Do you know him?" he asked.

She shook her head. "No, I simply heard one of the stories," she replied. *How much more sense that makes,* she thought to herself. She had not seen any sign of the gambler in Rivington, but it had seemed quite natural to endow him with all of the vices of a rake. For a moment, her conscience troubled her.

"Once again, Miss Howard, I present my suit. Now that you see that I have no need of your money and are assured that I will not gamble it away, will you marry me?"

She patted his cheek and laughed. "I believe that I may, my dear. My solicitor will speak with yours." She glanced about the rose garden. "Perhaps we shall marry this very week—here in the garden."

Rivington once more shook his head mournfully. "I see that you will call the tune, dear lady, but I am too old to run away. I fear that I must learn to dance to it."

Alexa smiled and led him deeper into the garden. "I believe, sir, that you will come to like it very well."

And out of sight of any prying eyes, they kissed, his lips lingering, his arms holding her firmly, reluctant to release her.

"I believe, ma'am, that you may be in the right of it—once again," he murmured, drawing her closer.

ABOUT THE AUTHOR

Mona Gedney lives with her family in West Lafayette, IN. She is the author of nine Zebra Regency romances. Mona loves to hear from readers, and you may write to her c/o Zebra Books. Please include a self-addressed stamped envelope if you wish a response.

THE ROMANTIC
BRIDE

NANCY LAWRENCE

When the door to the library opened, Miss Helen Worth looked up in a rather distracted fashion from the stacks of papers arrayed about the top of her desk and said, "Good morning, Papa. I shall speak with you presently if only I can get these numbers to tot correctly!"

Robert Worth, a man who gladly admitted to a limited mathematical ability of his own, made a face. "What's all this? Don't tell me you've taken it into your head to audit the home farm books again!"

"No, but I believe I have hit upon a method for irrigating the western lea. If my calculations are correct, we should be able to put that land to good use at last."

Mr. Worth frowned. "Here now, Helen, why do you insist upon involving yourself in such stuff and nonsense? We have a perfectly good man in Kendle to look after this sort of business on our behalf."

"Yes, Papa, but Mr. Kendle isn't of the opinion that the thing can be done. Oh, I know he would carry out my instructions if I gave them, but I think, if I show him these numbers and drawings, he will be convinced at last and will do the thing wholeheartedly. After all, it is difficult to argue with numbers."

Considering his own limited ability in that area, Mr. Worth thought it would be rather impossible. He picked up a sheet of paper and examined it with distaste. "I wish you would not spend quite so much of your time managing the estates."

"Papa, I have managed the estates these seven years at least. We agreed it would be so, for you have no head for these matters, while I do. Besides, I enjoy doing it."

"But wouldn't you rather spend your time in other ways? Attending parties or cozing with your friends or driving that new blue phaeton of yours about Town? I hate to think of you closeted away in this fashion when you might instead be enjoying a bit of London Society."

"Now, Papa," Helen said with the patience of a parent facing a recalcitrant child, "you know perfectly well that I do not closet myself away and that I enjoy a very lively social calendar. I have a good many friends and I am invited to every occasion of fashion." She gave her gold-brown curls a slight shake as she picked up her pen, intent upon resuming her work. "Really, Papa, sometimes I think you worry too much and too needlessly."

"There are those who will tell you I don't worry enough," her father muttered. He saw that she had once again turned her attention to the papers before her and said, "Here now, Helen, I wish you to put all your ciphers and plans aside for a moment. I have something to talk to you about—something that has weighed on my mind for some time."

Rather than giving her father her undivided attention, Helen continued to shuffle the papers on the desk and said, in a somewhat preoccupied fashion, "Mrs. Drayton-Kerr."

Her father started. "What did you say?"

"Mrs. Drayton-Kerr," Helen repeated obediently. "You said you wished to discuss something with me, and I merely assumed you wanted my opinion as to which of your many flirts you should drive in the park today. I cast my vote for Mrs. Drayton-Kerr. Out of all your lady friends, I like her most extremely." She looked up in time to see the confounded expression on her father's face. "That was the subject you wished to speak to me about, was it not?"

"No, indeed, it was not! What a very frippery fellow you must think me!"

"Not at all, Papa. I think you are a handsome and charming man whose company is much in demand. I merely assumed—"

"Incorrectly, my girl! You assumed most incorrectly indeed! It just so happens that I am here to discuss a matter of the greatest import!"

With very little effort, Helen conjured a catalogue of possible subjects her father might wish to discuss: the latest suit of clothes fitted for him by Weston; the sum of his winnings at faro the night before; whether or not he would ever be able to convince his good friend, Lord Bricknell, to sell his best 'Shire Hunter— all of these topics were, as her father had pointed out on many occasions, of eminent importance in his life.

In his usual mien, her father embarked upon each day with a breezy insouciance that was his trademark. He regularly avoided unpleasant issues that might provoke his temper and rarely succumbed to any inducement that might require him to form a serious thought.

Yet on this occasion, Helen saw that there was a slight crease between his brows and an odd twist to his normally placid lips. Gone was all trace of his usually elegant movement; instead, he was pacing rather uneasily across the carpeted floor in front of Helen's desk in a fashion she had never before witnessed. All told, his behavior was so uncharacteristic, so outside of her normal ken, that she was suddenly of the opinion that something must have gone seriously wrong indeed.

Forcing herself to remain calm, Helen set her pen down, folded her hands together atop a stack of now-forgotten papers, and said, "You have my attention, Papa. This sounds most serious indeed!"

"It is," her father said importantly. "Helen, I— I—! Dash it, I don't suppose there is any reason to dip this business in honey, so I shall just say it outright. Helen, I wish to speak to you of marriage!"

Of all the things Helen had imagined he might wish to discuss, that was one such subject she had never considered. "Marriage! Papa, are you certain?" she asked.

"I was never more certain in my life. As I said, I've given the matter a considerable amount of thought and my mind is entirely made up."

For a moment, Helen was at a loss to know what to say. At last, she summoned a slight, if rather forced, smile and went to him, her hands outstretched. "Then I am truly happy for you, Papa, and you have my best wishes. Only tell me who the fortunate lady is!"

He caught her hands. "No, no! You've got the thing all wrong! *I* am not the one to be married. *You are!*"

"Me?" she repeated with a slight laugh of surprise. "But I am not planning to be married at all."

"Yes, and that's the very thing that has me over a wheelbarrow."

She pulled her hands from his grasp and said warningly, "Now, Papa . . ."

"Helen, you're a beautiful girl, accomplished, graceful, intelligent. Yet you've seen still another birthday come and go without a husband. You're twenty-eight now, aren't you? Good God, child, what are you waiting for?"

"Papa, I am happy as I am," she said simply.

"Let me finish, Helen, for I've come to realize just how important a subject this is. That is why—for your own good, mind!—I have decided that you must be married before I die."

Helen gave a short gasp and her complexion paled slightly. "Papa! Never say it! Gracious, you aren't ill! There isn't anything . . ."

He halted her stumbling words with a negligent wave of his ringed hand. "Calm yourself! There's nothing wrong with me—at least, not that I'm aware of. But the thing is, Helen, that I'm not getting any younger. Oh, I don't plan to stick my spoon in the wall yet, but the deuce of it is that men younger than I, who were in much better health, have passed on ahead of me. Why, two months ago, Lord Edgefield died while dressing for dinner and ruined a perfectly good suit of clothes in the process. And just last week, Morris Butler cut up suddenly while seated at the faro table—and he was winning! I tell you, that sort of thing can make a man take notice."

"But, Papa, what does all of this have to do with the fact that I am not married?"

Mr. Worth didn't answer right away, but studied her a moment. At last, he said in a quiet, solemn voice, "I worry about you, my pet. I worry over what shall become of you once the day arrives that I am gone."

"But, Papa, nothing will happen to me. I suspect I shall carry on as I always have."

"Alone?" he asked rather pointedly.

There was something about the manner in which he said that single word that made her uncomfortable. "You are forgetting Aunt Minnie, who has shared our home, Papa, for as many years as I can recall."

"Your aunt Minnie won't see fifty again. She cannot live forever. What happens then?"

Helen moved away toward the window and absently picked at the fringe that adorned the draperies. "I cannot say I like the road this conversation has taken!'' she said with an overbright laugh, as if she hoped to dispel a sudden gloom with such a meager gesture.

''Unpleasant business, I know, but we cannot avoid it. Let me put it plainly before you, Helen. I'm a wealthy man, and once I am gone from this earth, there's a more than decent chance you shall be besieged by fortune hunters. They'll tell you how beautiful you are—which is nothing short of the truth, I admit!—and they'll ply you with compliments until they have convinced you to hand them your heart and your inheritance. I shouldn't wish for one of those scoundrels to bring you heartache, my dear.''

''I won't let them,'' she said with a hint of the self-assurance her father had always admired. ''Besides, you have never before cared that I am not married. You have never even broached this topic before.''

''Meaning that I'm not much of a father, eh? You might as well say it, for you'd be speaking nothing but the truth. God knows I was never quite sure how to raise a daughter!''

''Then allow me to be the first to tell you what an excellent business you made of it. You must have exceptional skill as a parent—only look at the result!'' Helen implored with an impish light in her blue eyes.

Her father didn't reply right away, but stood watching her for a moment. At last, he said, in an oddly thoughtful tone, ''Do you know, just now you looked to be the very image of your dear mother! How like her you are!''

Helen was thrown a bit off her stride, for her father

rarely displayed such tenderness. A small swell of emotion rose in her throat, but she managed to say, "That is quite the nicest thing you have ever said to me."

Mr. Worth reached over and trailed an affectionate finger down her soft cheek. "Then you deserve a better father, I daresay—one who will tell you often what a good daughter you are." He wrapped one arm about her shoulders and held her affectionately.

It was a comforting gesture, one that he had scarce performed in the years since Helen had put up her hair and let down her skirts and taken her place in the world as a grown woman.

Helen ran the tips of her fingers over the stiffly starched ruffle of his shirtfront and asked, "Papa, why are you suddenly so eager to see me married?"

"You mistake me. I wish to see you happy—there's a difference, you know."

"Then why all this talk of husbands?"

"Because one day I will be gone and your aunt Minnie will be gone, as well. On that day, you'll find yourself alone with only your estate plans and books to keep you company. I don't mind telling you that's a lonely life for a woman."

"But, Papa, in your heart of hearts, you wouldn't wish me to marry against my principles, would you?"

"And just what, exactly, are your principles, my pet?"

"Nothing extraordinary, I assure you. But when I do marry, I should like to marry for love. At the very least, I should like to feel a strong attachment to the gentleman before I pledge my life to him."

"That doesn't seem unreasonable."

"I thought so, too, but of all the gentlemen of my acquaintance, I have never felt any particular affection for any one man. Perhaps the reason is that I have simply not yet met the man who is the right match for me."

"Or perhaps you ask too much. Sometimes, the affection comes after the marriage has begun, you know."

Helen frowned slightly. "I do not think that is how it was for you and Mama."

"You are half right. Your mother was already in love with me by the time she donned her wedding clothes, while I learned to love her over time. Still, no man can argue that ours was not a happy marriage."

That revelation came as a complete surprise to Helen. She had always known her parents loved each other, and she had long suspected that the profound affection they shared was the underlying reason that her father had never remarried after his wife's death. Never had she suspected that such a love had not been perfect from the first.

Helen gave her head a slight shake. "Papa, are you certain? Truly, you did not love Mama when you married her?"

"My oath on it."

"But you did learn to love her at last?"

"With all my heart," Mr. Worth vowed simply.

"Then I am amazed, for though I have few memories of Mama, I remember one occasion most distinctly. She held me very close and told me that I should never marry unless the man I wed pledged to love me truly, madly, and deeply. I never forgot the lesson, Papa, and I always thought that, until I could meet such a man as Mama described, I would be content to live my life with you and Aunt Minnie." She looked up then and saw a rather odd expression on her father's face. She said ruefully, "Now you shall think me silly and overly romantic."

"Not at all, but I should hate to see you give up a chance for happiness because of an ideal."

"A chance for happiness? Papa, you forget that no gentleman has yet offered for me."

"And there you are wrong, for a young man has done so this very day."

Her eyes widened in surprise. "I don't believe it! Who could have done so?"

"Can you not guess?"

"I haven't the vaguest notion. There is no man of my acquaintance who has shown the least partiality to me—at least, no man whose regard I return."

"Then I suppose you would be astonished to know the Addison boy wishes to make you an offer?"

"Charles Addison?" Helen asked, her blue eyes wide with surprise. "I never suspected he had marriage on his mind."

"On his mind and ready to speak on it. Helen, I think you should accept his suit."

She hesitated only a moment before replying, "But, Papa, I do not love him."

"My pet, I would much rather see you live your days with a companion you respect than alone with your ideals."

He would have said more, but there was a rap on the door and Minerva Worth entered the room.

She came to them in a rustle of watered silk and a faint cloud of lilac perfume and smiled happily upon them, saying, "I thought I heard you in here. May I come in? I am off to visit poor Lady Edgefield, Helen, and thought you might like to accompany me."

"Minnie, mind your manners," Mr. Worth boomed. "You have intruded upon a very private conversation! Helen and I were just in the middle of—" He stopped short as a notion came to him.

He strode across the room to the door and caught his sister-in-law by the elbow just as she was about to beat a hasty retreat back into the hall. He brought her back into the room, saying, "No, no, don't leave! My mistake, Minnie. Of course you must join us! Why, you are, after all, a part of this family."

"I would never dream of intruding, Robert," she said, anxiously. "If you and Helen wish to be alone—"

"Not at all! In fact, I'm glad you've joined us. We were just speaking of marriage."

Minnie cast a wide-eyed look from his face to Helen's. "Indeed? Whose?"

"Why, Helen's, of course. I mean to have her accept the Addison boy."

"Goodness! Has he offered for you, my dear?" Minnie asked, reaching over to clasp Helen's hand.

"Papa says he has, although I am not at all sure why he should. He doesn't love me nor do I hold the least affection for him!"

"And that's why I want you to talk to her, Minnie," Mr. Worth said. "Tell Helen all about love and marriage. After all, you married that worthless fribble of a brother of mine for love, didn't you? And look at you now! Living off the kindness of relatives and depending upon your brother-in-law for pin money! Tell Helen what a mistake your marriage was!"

Minnie's face paled. "Robert, I wish you wouldn't speak so!"

"Come, you wouldn't be telling Helen anything she doesn't already know!"

"Papa, you are being quite cruel," Helen said severely.

"Am I? I didn't mean to be so," he said in his candid way. "I only wish you to understand, my pet, that even a marriage made in love can be disastrous. Apply to your aunt Minnie if you don't believe me!"

After years of living with her brother-in-law, Minnie had long become inured to his brash way of speaking. She looked up at Helen and said simply, "My dear, you must simply do what you think is best."

"Pleasing her papa is best!" Mr. Worth said.

"But I don't love him!" Helen clasped her aunt's hand in a meaningful grip. "Dear Aunt Minnie, I do not wish to marry where there is no love. My mama would not have wanted me to. She told me I mustn't marry unless the gentleman is truly, madly, and deeply in love with me."

"I know," Minnie said, "for I was there when she told you so. But you must remember, too, my dear, that as a general rule that sort of love never comes to a person. Few people are as passionate as your mother was, I fear."

"It's true," Mr. Worth said solemnly. "Your mother was a woman of deep feeling. You, on the other hand, are a sensible girl and not at all prone to romantic notions, as your mother was."

"Perhaps I should be," Helen said stubbornly. "You have always told me how wonderful she was, and I have tried to be like her."

"You can be. Marry and set up your house and fill your nurseries. You'll prove to be a good mother, just as she did," her father recommended.

Helen took a few nervous steps about the room. She had always thought she knew her own mind; she had always been content with her life. But now it seemed that her father was encouraging her to decide upon a course of action she would much rather avoid. He was pressuring her, imposing his will upon her in such a way that she didn't know what to think. She turned beseeching eyes upon her aunt. "Aunt Minnie? What have you to say of all this?"

"My dear, I cannot advise you. But you would be wise, I think, to remember that your father loves you and only wants what is best for you."

"The Addison boy is a fine young man," insisted Mr. Worth. "He's bright and comes of a good family. What's more, he likes you. I could trust a man like him to be good to you, my pet."

Now it only remained for Helen to decide she could trust him, as well. She had always wanted marriage and in her twenty-eight years had often longed for children of her own; yet she had set aside that longing to follow her mother's wishes. Charles Addison was not the first man to offer her marriage; but, she realized with a slight feeling of alarm, he might be the last man to do so. She had never loved any of the men who had proposed marriage to her over the years, but she did like Charles. He was far from the husband of her dreams, but she believed wholeheartedly that, of all the men of her acquaintance, he would undoubtedly make the most acceptable husband.

"Papa," she said tentatively, "are you certain he wishes to marry me?"

"I had it from his very lips this morning. And you must know that his father and I have been right and tight for many years. Nothing would make the two of us happier than to see our children married."

Once again, Helen moved to the window and stared out at the gardens while she tried to make sense of her feelings. She had clung to that memory of her mother and the advice she had given for so long that she was hard pressed to ignore it now. Yet Helen's sensible nature told her that her father was right: She was waiting for a love that might never happen, and she was on the brink of declining what might prove to be her last chance at marrying and having a family of her own.

Solid, sensible Helen tamped down the last spark of the romantic ideal she had long carried in her heart. She looked over at her father. "Would my marrying Charles Addison please you that much, Papa?"

After twenty-eight years as Helen's father, Robert Worth was very well acquainted with that expression on her face. He smiled broadly and went to her with his arms outstretched. "Indeed it would!" he exclaimed, folding her into his embrace. "Minnie, we are about to plan a wedding for my pet. What say we make it a June wedding, eh?''

By the third week of May, Helen's wedding plans were well underway. The banns had been read and her father had placed an announcement of her betrothal in *The Times*. Aunt Minnie had accompanied her to a shop on Bond Street, where they selected cards of invitation to the wedding breakfast, and in between trips to the modiste to be fitted for her wedding trousseau, Helen spent her time with Minnie addressing the invitations and posting them.

Since the day their betrothal was announced, Helen and Charles had begun to spend a considerable amount of time together. She found she liked him very well and learned to feel quite comfortable in his presence. For his part, Charles proved to be polite and attentive. Helen would have liked him to speak every once in a while of his feelings for her, but he made no attempt to do so. Upon reflection, Helen considered that it was just as well, for she recognized that her feelings for Charles were not at all profound or deep. Still, the couple was seen everywhere together, a fact that pleased her father and made Minnie look upon her with soulful eyes and reminisce about her own long-ago marriage.

In the library, Helen regularly engaged in sorting through the stacks of newly delivered invitations to the Season's most fashionable events. Her aunt found her there one afternoon and came upon her in a flutter of excitement.

"My dear, you must come quickly. Charles Addison has called and is waiting for you in the drawing room. He was most insistent that he see you right away and said that, if you were not at home, he should not leave until he saw you!"

Helen left her chair behind the desk and shook out her skirts. "I wonder what he could mean by such a statement?"

"Perhaps his feelings for you run much more deeply than we ever gave him credit for," suggested Minnie, ever the romantic.

"Or perhaps he merely wishes to cry off attending Lady Bricknell's ball this evening. We have, I believe, been out until all hours every night this past week. I never knew a betrothal could be so exhausting!"

Helen drew her shawl up about her slim shoulders and left the library in good spirits. She returned not twenty minutes later in a state that bordered on shock.

Minnie was there, having tarried to select a book from the shelves, and saw, when the door opened and her niece entered the room, that Helen's hands seemed to be trembling slightly and that her face had gone rather pale.

"Helen dear, you look as though you have suffered something of a shock! Tell me, is anything amiss?"

Helen sat limply down behind the desk and brought her trembling fingertips up to cover her mouth. It took several minutes for her to compel her mind to answer. At last, she said, "I have just spoken with Charles—Mr. Addison! He said— That is, he wished to tell me—" She stopped, then marshaled her composure and said, with a short, nervous laugh, "Charles Addison has told me he cannot marry me, after all!"

Minnie gasped. "He could never have said so!"

"He did. Quite eloquently, as a matter of fact. It seems he has—" She paused while she tried to gain control over her lower lip, which had begun to tremble threateningly. "He said he has fallen in love. He fears he cannot go through with a marriage to me when his affections are engaged elsewhere."

"The beast!" Minnie breathed. "Only wait until your papa hears of this!"

"No!" Helen said firmly. "Charles is quite correct. I should not wish to marry a man who loves another." She could not compel her brain to form more words, but no sooner had she abandoned any further attempts at speech than she felt tears prick at the backs of her eyes.

She looked blindly out the window; the shawl about her arms weighed as heavily as if it had been made of lead. She sat thus, near to tears but unable to cry, wishing she could tell her aunt what she was feeling, but unable to summon any words past her lips.

After a few moments, the door was flung open. Through eyes blurred with tears, Helen saw her father enter the room. She couldn't see him clearly, but she had an impression that his normally handsome face had contorted into a mask of distress. He marched up to her without hesitation and drew her from the chair to wrap his arms protectively about her.

"My pet!" he murmured soothingly. "I came as soon as I heard the news!"

Those gentle words and the comfort of his embrace

proved to be Helen's undoing. At last the tears spilled over, and she exclaimed in a watery voice, "Oh, Papa! I am thoroughly and utterly ruined!"

A week later, Helen was still excusing herself from leaving the house. She declined on more than one occasion to bear her aunt company while she paid morning calls, and on still another afternoon she claimed a headache rather than present herself downstairs to the circle of ladies who met regularly in her aunt's drawing room for tea and conversation.

Her father, who confessed in a momentary display of weakness that he held himself wholly responsible for the turn of events, gave up trying to entice Helen to drive her blue phaeton about town as she used to.

Instead, Helen spent her days in a solitary state, feeling deeply injured and unable to concentrate on either the most entertaining novel or important estate record.

Minnie came upon her in the library one afternoon. Helen was seated behind the desk, and at first glance, Minnie thought the dear girl might at last be showing signs of returning to her old self. A stack of papers was arrayed upon the desktop, and a pen was poised between Helen's gracefully tapered fingers. Further inspection, however, proved that Helen's attention was focused upon the scene outside the window, the papers were wholly ignored, and the pen, long forgotten, had dribbled a permanent blotch of ink upon her skirt.

Minnie called the damage to Helen's attention.

"It's only a dress, Aunt," said Helen with a slight shrug. "I daresay it doesn't signify."

Since Helen had long taken pride in possessing the finest fashions to be had from London's grandest couturier, that comment caused her aunt no small degree of alarm. "Helen Worth, I cannot sit idly by and watch you behave so!" she said severely. "My dear girl, you simply cannot go on this way!"

Helen's blue eyes, which had once been alive with spirit, looked upon her aunt with an alarming lack of emotion. "Please don't scold me, Aunt," she said in a small voice. "I don't think I could bear it."

Now thoroughly alarmed, Minnie drew Helen from her chair. With a firm hold upon her niece's wrist, she drew her out into the hall and up the stairs to her bedchamber.

Minnie threw open the door to the wardrobe, revealing a row of new gowns, which had been fitted and delivered for Helen's wedding trip. The mere sight of them was enough to make Helen look away.

"I want you to change your dress, Helen," her aunt commanded, "for you are expecting callers."

"Me? But no one has wished to call upon me since—" She broke off, unwilling to even mention that fateful day one week past.

"The ladies have been asking for you," said Minnie, referring to the group of women who had made it a practice over the course of many years to gather on a weekly basis in the Worth drawing room.

"No, Aunt, I couldn't see them. Please don't ask me to!" implored Helen.

"My dear, you are being overly dramatic, I think.

The ladies are your friends and have been for some time. I believe you once told me that you especially liked Mrs. Drayton-Kerr. She most particularly asked about you the last time she was here."

Helen shook her head. "I cannot face them."

"Why? What is it you fear will happen? Do you think a lady of Mrs. Drayton-Kerr's disposition will laugh at you? Or perhaps you fear that she will rudely question you over the events of the last week?"

"No, Aunt, I don't fear either of those things."

"What then? Why will you not come and sit with old friends and share a dish of tea?"

When Minnie put it in those terms, Helen could not very well argue with her aunt. She knew only that the mortifying circumstances of the last week had left her unwilling to see anyone.

Aunt Minnie patted her hand encouragingly. "Why don't you change your dress and come down to the drawing room? Of a certain, you shall be glad you did."

Helen did not share her aunt's certainty, but left alone in her bedchamber, she was honest enough to admit that her Minnie was right about one thing: She could not go on as she was. In the last week she had, she thought, become almost a different person: jittery and skittish and possessing not the least trace of the confidence that had once been her hallmark. She didn't much care for the person she had become. Even less did she care to think of herself living the remainder of her days cowering in her room, fearful of going about in public. She took a deep breath and rang for her maid.

In less than half an hour, Helen presented herself, freshly gowned and coiffed, in the drawing room. She entered the room to find her aunt Minnie entertaining the same group of ladies who had, from week to week, watched Helen grow up. She immediately recognized many of them, including Mrs. Drayton-Kerr, a stylish woman of beauty and wit who had long harbored feelings of affection for Helen's father. She was engaged in conversation; a smile was on her lips and a delicate teacup and saucer were poised in her hand. Upon Helen's entrance, she looked up, and her gaze met Helen's. Her conversation died away and her face underwent a transformation; her smile vanished, and in her eyes, which had only a moment before been bright with pleasure, Helen read compassion and a healthy dose of pity.

Quickly, Helen looked away, only to find that the other ladies in the room bore the very same expression. The wretched heat of embarrassment began its slow and steady climb up her neck and she prayed that no one would notice.

Aunt Minnie cast her an encouraging smile and patted the seat cushion next to her. "Ah, Helen! How nice. Come here, my dear, and join us."

Helen moved to obey, but by the time she was seated beside Minnie, she was deeply aware that each woman present was assessing her in silence.

At last, Mrs. Drayton-Kerr, who Helen had long thought to be a woman of impeccable manners, broke the awkward silence, saying, "We were just speaking of the dinner party I shall hold later this week. Your aunt has told us, dear Helen, that you have been feeling not quite the thing. I hope you shall be well enough by Thursday night to attend.''

"Oh, yes, do," one of the other ladies said encouragingly. "Such a gay affair it will be! So many beautiful ladies, so many handsome young men! Perhaps we shall prevail upon Mrs. Drayton-Kerr to roll up the carpet in one of her rooms and allow you young people to dance. I am certain one of the gentlemen will be happy to partner you for the evening, Helen."

"I believe," yet another woman said, "Lord Bridgestone is yet unattached."

Since it was common knowledge that Lord Bridgestone, a widower well past sixty summers, had over the course of time unsuccessfully offered for virtually every young woman of marriageable age, Helen was a little alarmed by such a suggestion.

So was the first woman who spoke, for she retorted, "Oh, posh! Helen can do much better than Lord Bridgestone. We shall simply have to ply our minds to the task of finding the right young man, won't we, Helen?"

She again knew the uncomfortable feeling of having all the ladies in the room regard her at once. She couldn't bear it. She knew the ladies meant well and knew, too, that they were kindly attempting to help her put her life back in order; yet it was a hurtful realization to find herself the object of such pity. She had always been independent, secure, and confident in the knowledge that she was an attractive woman with a life that was fulfilling and happy. That confidence was now seriously shaken. In fact, she rather thought that the ladies could not have felt more sorry for her if her back were suddenly to twist into a hump and the tip of her nose were to erupt in a wart.

The ladies sat watching her in expectant silence, but no words of reply came to her lips, no gracious response formed in her throat. All she could think of was the humiliation of her circumstance, that in their zeal to be sympathetic the ladies were speaking almost as if she weren't even in the room.

It was all too much. Helen felt tears forming in her eyes and knew she had to escape before she dissolved into a puddle of utter foolishness. She barely managed to utter a stumbling excuse before she fled the room and sought refuge in her bedchamber.

The tears she shed came more from impotent frustration than sorrow; they lasted only long enough to bring a rather becoming flush to her cheeks and a slight trace of puffiness to her blue eyes. She was dabbing a linen kerchief to the last of her tears when a knock sounded at her door and her aunt entered the room.

"Don't say it!" Helen begged. "I know my behavior was horrid. I know, too, that I should march right back down to the drawing room and beg the forgiveness of every one of those ladies. Oh, but, Aunt, I cannot bring myself to do it!"

She had meant to be composed and collected, but no sooner had she finished speaking than she was again close to tears. Once more did she put into use the lace-trimmed kerchief.

"My poor Helen," Minnie uttered as she wrapped a sympathetic arm about her niece's shoulders and led her over to sit upon the bed. "Dearest, why so many tears? You told me you held not the least degree of affection for Charles Addison, yet for the past week, you have cried as if your heart were broken."

"It is not my heart that is broken, Aunt, but my self-esteem. I cannot bear to be looked upon with pity! I know your friends were trying to be kind, but the manner in which they looked at me! And when they suggested Lord Bridgestone as a suitable partner, I was never more humiliated in my life!"

"My dear, this is most unlike you," Minnie said as she gave Helen's shoulder a comforting squeeze. "You have always been a girl of character and self-possession with a confidence I admire."

"That girl is gone forever," Helen said with a hint of the dramatic.

"You'll recover soon enough, as will your reputation, I think. In the meantime, you must carry on. It would never do for you to let the *ton* think for one moment you have been defeated."

"But I have been, Aunt Minnie," Helen said in a forlorn voice from behind her kerchief. "I have been utterly and irrevocably vanquished and I haven't the least notion how I shall live through this!"

"Nonsense! I won't hear you speak in such a fashion!" her aunt said bracingly. "Now you listen to me, Helen Worth, for I shall tell you how you will live. You will hold your head up high, and you will attend every ball, every party for which you received a card of invitation. And you shall attend each event dressed in your finest gown and wearing your brightest smile!"

To Helen's way of thinking, Aunt Minnie had no

idea what she was asking. "How can I ever do such a thing? Those invitations were issued to both Charles and me. We were invited as a betrothed couple. I couldn't possibly attend those balls and routs alone!"

"Then you must attend with an escort," Aunt Minnie replied promptly, "and I know the very young man to perform such a service. His mother was a friend of your mother's, God rest her soul, and of mine. My dear, I am speaking of Edmond Manwaring."

Helen emerged from behind her kerchief to cast her aunt a look of abject horror. "Edmond Manwaring?"

"Yes, indeed, my dear. He is in London and spoke to your father not two nights ago at his club. He asked after you and wondered aloud to your father whether or not you might remember him."

"Do I remember Edmond Manwaring?" Helen asked in a tone of alarm. "He was so horrid, it is unlikely I shall ever forget him!"

Aunt Minnie paled slightly. "Why, Helen, what an awful thing to say!"

"Dearest Aunt, you cannot be sincere! Edmond Manwaring was a horrid little boy and the scourge of the neighborhood when we were children. He was spoiled, undisciplined, and nothing short of incorrigible!"

"But, Helen dear, he's not a child anymore," Aunt Minnie said reasonably. "He'd be a grown man by now. I'm certain he has changed."

Helen was of the opinion that no degree of change in Edmond Manwaring could ever be enough. She had two very clear memories of Evil Edmond. She had been sixteen when Edmond's mother had died and eighteen when Edmond's father had taken him away to live with his grandmother in Derbyshire. In those days, he had been an impossibly scrawny boy, two years younger than she, who was little more than a collection of gangly arms and long legs and a disposition that drove him to mercilessly tease and torment the other children. Even now, Helen was able to recall with alarming clarity some of the ideas spawned by Evil Edmond's horrifying imagination.

Yet somehow, Helen had felt a bit protective of him. She recalled the look that had been in his eyes in the days and weeks after his mother died. He had been most unlike himself, somehow softer and infinitely more vulnerable. Some of the neighborhood children who had long been victims of his childish treacheries had seen in Edmond's sorrow an opportunity to avenge themselves with teasings, but Helen had stepped in and assumed the role of protectress. That act of compassion had earned her some teasing of her own, but she hadn't minded. Every time Evil Edmond had looked at her with those blue eyes of his filled with gratitude, she had felt a spark of affection for him.

But any such spark had long since faded. She had no intention of renewing an acquaintance with Edmond Manwaring, whether he had grown or not. She searched her resourceful imagination for a reason to decline her aunt's suggestion. "Perhaps it would not be a good idea for me to be seen in public with a gentleman so soon after severing my betrothal to Charles."

"Then I shall simply invite Edmond to dine with us one evening. After all, he is an old friend of the family!"

Helen's eyes widened in alarm. Dinner with Edmond Manwaring? She'd rather eat worms. In fact, she distinctly remembered a time when Evil Edmond had chased her through the sitting room with a handful of the squiggly things. She almost shuddered at the memory.

"Dearest aunt, I beg you will not do so—at least, not quite yet," Helen said firmly. She saw the look of disappointment in her aunt's eyes, and she clasped her hand in an affectionate grip. "I know you have only my welfare at heart and I know you only wish the best for me. I shall do as you suggest and shall venture out into Society and I shall hold my head up high. But, dear aunt, do not, I beg you, seek to fix my interest with another young man. Leave me, please, to be content as I am."

Helen kept her promise to her aunt. Over the course of the next three nights, she attended one card party, one drum, and a musicale. At each, she performed as naturally as she was able, with a smile on her lips and her head held high. She was deeply aware that at each function she was the object of some rather potent stares and that ladies of fashion whispered about her from behind the muffling effects of their painted fans. Such actions were hurtful and on the carriage ride home she railed against the injustice of it all to her aunt. But a promise was a promise, and on the very next evening, Helen ventured out yet again, her head still held high and that smile of polite pleasure still fixed upon her lips.

On Thursday evening, Helen rode out with her father and aunt to attend Mrs. Drayton-Kerr's dinner party. It was a small affair by the standards of the *ton*. The table was set for twenty places, and only the most glittering persons and dearest friends of their hostess were fortunate enough to garner an invitation to dine. Several dozen more guests arrived after dinner to play cards and converse to the accompaniment of a small orchestra.

A circle of young men and women gravitated toward Helen's side. She was on familiar footings with each of them, having moved in the same social circle for some years, and for a short while, she was able to forget her troubles and revel in their friendship.

One of her friends petitioned Mrs. Drayton-Kerr to take up the rugs and order the orchestra to play music suitable for dancing. Before long, there were neat rows of men and women making their way down the center of the room in time to the music of a lively country dance.

From her position near the far side of the room, Helen commanded a full view of both the festivities and of the doorway. When her attention was not claimed in conversation or focused upon the couples dancing before her, she was able to watch the guests as they arrived. She knew them all, of course, for the Worth family moved in a wide and rather elite circle of friends and acquaintances, and Helen was on familiar terms with virtually every person in attendance.

Or so she thought. A young man who arrived rather late, just as her hostess was abandoning her position by the door, proved to be wholly unknown to Helen. She watched as the man shook hands with her hostess and engaged her in a conversation that reduced the poor woman to little more than a giggling girl.

He was certainly a very striking man possessed of a good deal of charm. He was of average height and well proportioned, with broad, strong shoulders, a pair of muscular legs, and a grace of movement that Helen rather thought she could watch with pleasure for hours at a time.

But it was his countenance that most captured her attention. His nose was straight, and his finely formed lips parted in a smile over even white teeth. His hair was dark, almost black in color, and fell appealingly across his forehead above a pair of crystal blue eyes.

All told, the effect of his appearance was overwhelmingly handsome and Helen realized that she was unabashedly staring at the man.

She jerked her attention back toward her companions and tried to pick up the thread of their conversation, but in a very little while, she found her gaze wandering of its own volition back toward the door, in search of the gentleman with the startling blue eyes.

He was not to be found. Indeed, he had disappeared into the throng of guests, and Helen found herself feeling a little disappointed. She shifted her posture slightly and did her best to look about the room with a casual unconcern, hoping that she might catch yet another glimpse of the man. She caught, instead, her aunt's attention and drew her a little apart from the other guests.

"Aunt, there is a stranger in attendance tonight, a gentleman I do not know."

Minnie looked doubtful. "I cannot think who you may mean. We are well acquainted, I think, with everyone here."

"I know what I saw," Helen insisted. "A man arrived not very long ago. I saw him speaking with Mrs. Drayton-Kerr."

"Dear child, forget the stranger!" Aunt Minnie said, brushing aside Helen's curiosity with a negligent wave of her hand. "Only guess who is in attendance this evening!"

Judging by the sudden flush on her aunt's cheeks and the sound of her aunt's voice, Helen rather thought that a member of the royal family had just arrived. "Someone of importance, I should think. Tell me, Aunt, who is in attendance?"

Aunt Minnie paused dramatically. "Edmond Manwaring!"

Helen couldn't have been more disappointed, but that emotion was quickly replaced by a feeling of impending doom. For the last week, Helen had done her best to avoid any opportunity to reacquaint herself with Edmond Manwaring. Her aunt had brought his name up several times in various conversations, and in each instance, Helen was able to parry Minnie's efforts to orchestrate a reunion with Edmond. Thus far, Helen had successfully avoided meeting the grown-up equivalent of the horrid little boy from her childhood, but now it appeared that she would have to suffer his attentions after all and that she would be made to do so in a public setting among friends and acquaintances.

"Perhaps," Aunt Minnie said in a hopeful tone, "you will allow Edmond to take you in to supper?"

Helen felt a small trill of alarm run up her spine. The Edmond Manwaring of her memory wasn't above tripping servants or engaging in food fights, even in the best dining room in London. Allowing him to escort her to supper would be inviting trouble.

Her eyes scanned the crowded room. In the far corner stood a young man, awkward in appearance, lacking in conversation with those about him, and overdressed, even by a dandy's standards. He turned his head and his bespectacled eyes met hers. He smiled slightly and Helen felt her stomach lurch. *Edmond!*

She turned quickly about, lest the young man in the corner should recognize her from their days as children and form the notion that he was welcome to seek her out.

Fighting back a growing sense of panic, she implored, "Dearest Aunt, you cannot mean that I should speak to Edmond! Not *now!*"

"But, Helen, I have already spoken to him and he knows you are here. He is most anxious to renew his acquaintance with you, my dear."

Helen shook her head in a slight, but insistent, movement. "Please, Aunt, let us do as you suggested and invite him to dine with us as a family. That way, we shall be quite alone and no one of our acquaintance shall be about."

"If that is your wish," Minnie said doubtfully, "I suppose Edmond will understand."

Helen wasn't certain she understood her own actions herself. She knew her manner was ungracious and her actions unkind, but she also knew that she was unwilling to allow herself to become the object of any further gossip. Society had witnessed her betrothal and Society had observed her mortifying breakup with the man who had pledged to marry her. And now Aunt Minnie was proposing that Society witness her pursuit by a man of Evil Edmond Manwaring's caliber. That was a humiliation Helen was unwilling to allow.

Her eyes scanned the room as if seeking out possible avenues of escape. A short distance away she saw her father and Mrs. Drayton-Kerr engaged in conversation with the handsome man Helen had noticed earlier. They were smiling good-naturedly, and after a moment of conversation, she saw the young man look up and his gaze settled upon her.

She didn't know what to do. To be caught staring at the young man was nothing short of embarrassing, yet to discover that his gaze had sought her out was altogether flattering. After a moment, he looked away, leaving Helen with an overwhelming need to discover his identity.

It would have been a simple matter for her to march right up to her father and Mrs. Drayton-Kerr and secure an introduction to the handsome young man. With little effort, she thought, she could accomplish the deed. She had only to join their group with all the naturalness of a daughter who merely wished to exchange a few words with her own father. Surely no one would fault her for that; surely no one would suspect that she was angling for an introduction to the handsome stranger.

As she watched, her father laughed and gave the man's broad shoulder a good-natured clap. They seemed to be on most excellent terms with each other, a fact that only heightened Helen's already over-whelming curiosity. She was about to succumb to temptation and join them under some pretext when her aunt, still at her side, recalled her attention, saying, "Helen dear, will you not speak to him?"

Reluctantly, Helen drew her gaze back to her aunt. "Speak to him?" she repeated, her thoughts else-where.

"Helen, I don't believe you have listened to a word I've said. I wish you would pay attention, for Edmond is a very nice young man and I think the two of you would go on famously. Please, will you not at least speak to him?"

Instinctively, Helen knew that the only way to dis-pose of the subject of Edmond Manwaring, once and for all, was to agree at last to speak to the man. Then, perhaps, her aunt would be satisfied; then her aunt might be less inclined to push them together as she had been doing.

"Yes, I'll speak to Edmond," Helen said, resigned to her fate.

She found the young dandy in an anteroom where an array of refreshments was served. He was standing by one of the tables, quite alone, and had just finished arranging a quantity of food upon a plate, which he balanced in one hand. Then he accepted from a servant a cup of punch, which he held in the other. A small dollop of cream had dribbled down one side of his mouth, and Helen watched as he dashed it away with the cuff of his coat sleeve.

Helen took a deep breath to summon the courage she would need to make polite conversation with such a man. She squared her shoulders and was about to approach him when she heard a voice from behind say her name.

"Helen? Helen, is that you?"

The voice was deep and masculine, with a rich, clear quality that immediately commanded her attention. She turned and found herself looking up into the crystal blue eyes of the stranger—the very same gentleman she had admired earlier.

For a moment, she was a little surprised that he knew her name, but at last she said, as she continued to stare unabashedly up into his eyes, "Yes, I am Helen Worth."

The stranger took her hand between both of his own in a gesture she found at once comforting and exhilarating. "I thought I should recognize you anywhere. Helen, don't you know me? I am Edmond Manwaring."

Helen couldn't have been more stunned. She knew she should say something but no words came to mind. She merely stood staring up at him, mesmerized by the features of his face, which were oddly familiar, yet not at all like those she remembered.

Somehow, Edmond Manwaring had grown into a very attractive man. Gone were the gawky limbs, the oversize shoes, and the rough demeanor. Evil Edmond Manwaring, once the bane of the neighborhood children, had grown into a handsome, self-assured, and terribly attractive man.

"I don't believe it," she murmured in wonder and realized too late the rudeness of her remark.

He laughed good-naturedly. "Believe it! Evil Edmond is standing before you!"

She was a little mortified to realize he was aware of the nickname she had given him as a child. But his laugh was a little contagious, and she found herself responding to it. She looked up into his face. His eyes were bright, his lips were parted in a rather dazzling smile, and his dark brows were raised slightly in question.

"I suppose the proper thing for me to do would be to take you back to join your friends, but I would rather not do so just yet." Edmond extended his arm. "Will you take a turn with me about the room, Helen?"

She was having a hard time equating his clear, rich voice with the annoying squeak that had always come out of the mouth of Evil Edmond. Without thinking, she slipped her gloved hand into the crook of his arm and allowed him to lead her in a slow perambulation about the perimeter of the room.

Their travels took them past several acquaintances, and Helen performed all the necessary introductions as if in a dream. She watched as Edmond shook hands or executed a dignified bow, as the circumstances dictated, and noted how gracefully he moved and how easily his manner and conversation flowed.

Edmond led Helen off again. They had taken a few steps when he looked down at her and said, "I hope I am acquitting myself admirably."

His remark surprised her. "Of course! Why would you think otherwise?"

"Because you have been watching me most intently for the better part of the last ten minutes. Are you worried I shall do something unpleasant?"

Helen felt the dull heat of a blush cover her face. She *had* been staring, but only because she couldn't quite grasp the fact that this attractive man was the very same person who had so terrorized the neighborhood as a child.

"I have been staring at you, haven't I? Please forgive me, Mr. Manwaring, but I can scarcely believe it's you! You simply do not look like the same little boy I remembered."

"And you don't look the way I remember either," he said, looking down at her. "You're even lovelier now than you were at sixteen."

Helen felt herself blush and thankfully blessed the ballroom lighting, which cast enough shadows so he wouldn't notice her flushed face.

"Please do not think me rude, Mr. Manwaring, but—"

"Edmond," he said in a tone of gentle reproval. "You must call me Edmond, just as you did when we were children and were very much as brother and sister."

"Very well," she said in a calm tone, despite the

fact that she once again felt that traitorous blush creep up her neck. "Edmond."

"That's better. Now, what is it you wished to know?"

"You shall think me rude," she warned.

"Not at all."

"Then explain to me what happened? You are nothing like the Edmond Manwaring of my memory! What occurred to bring about such a transformation?"

Edmond smiled again, and Helen thought that he appeared to be enjoying himself—or perhaps he was simply enjoying her confusion. "The only thing that transformed me was time. I grew up."

"But your manners are so pleasing—"

"You can thank my grandmother for that. She didn't much tolerate my pranks and high jinks after I went to live with her."

"And your demeanor is so polished."

"My father insisted I take the Grand Tour and gain a little refinement. In other words, I simply grew up. It had to happen someday, you know."

True enough, Helen thought, but she had never suspected that it would happen in such pleasing proportions. Of all the boys and young men she had ever met in the course of her life, Edmond Manwaring was the one boy she had least expected to grow up into such a perfect young man.

At least, he appeared perfect on the surface, but she half suspected that in his breast beat the devious heart that had long ago earned him the epithet of Evil Edmond. At any moment, she feared a frog would jump from the pocket of his impeccably tailored coat, or he might wipe a gloved hand across his handsome cheek and leave a smudge of soot behind.

He led her to where Aunt Minnie was standing, plying her fan. She watched their approach with a smile of great satisfaction, then said, "So you are reacquainted at last! How splendid!"

"It has been my pleasure," Edmond said politely. "But I don't think Helen is yet convinced I can behave sensibly in public."

"On the contrary, I am most impressed!" she countered hastily. "You are a creditable escort, Edmond."

Aunt Minnie smiled with satisfaction. "He is indeed. I don't suppose, Edmond, we may impose upon you to lend us your arm at one function or another this Season?"

"Nothing would give me more pleasure, ma'am."

"And if ever Helen were in need of a dance partner," Minnie pursued, "I hope she may rely upon you to fill that position."

"Aunt!" Helen exclaimed, recognizing Minnie's shameful attempt to throw them together.

Edmond's lips slanted into a slight smile, but if he was aware, as Helen was, of Minnie's efforts, he did not show it. He said smoothly, "It shall be my pleasure. Helen, you have only to command me."

He courteously excused himself then; no sooner was he out of earshot than Minnie said wistfully, "I was so hoping he would ask you to dance, my dear."

"I am embarrassingly aware of that," her niece said dryly. "Aunt, it was wrong of you to speak as you did."

"Do you think Edmond did not wish to dance?"

"I rather think he doesn't know how."

Minnie frowned. "That hardly seems likely, my dear."

"Does it? Only consider! Edmond Manwaring was the least elegant boy of our acquaintance. His feet were enormous, and he was forever falling down from tree limbs and skinning a knee or tripping over rocks and scuffing his hands."

"My dear, I do not believe the size of a man's feet has anything to do with his ability to dance," her aunt said doubtfully.

"Perhaps not, but I think we would have a better chance of finding a fish driving a curricle than we have of finding Edmond Manwaring dancing credibly in a ballroom!"

Edmond called at Worth House just after the noon hour the next day. Helen received word of his arrival in her bedchamber, where she was applying the final touches to her daily toilette. No sooner had she heard his name announced than a vision of his handsome face and a memory of his deep voice sprang to mind. She went downstairs quickly, but before entering the drawing room, she paused to inspect her appearance one final time in a gilt-edged looking glass that hung in the hall.

In a moment of sheer vanity, she pinched at her cheeks and ran her tongue across her front teeth. It wasn't until she caught herself smoothing the faintest of wrinkles from her skirt that she realized that she was in a state of almost nervous anticipation over Edmond's visit.

For heaven's sake, she thought with a healthy mixture of alarm and disgust, *I am about to make an utter fool of myself!* She forced herself to present a placid and regal picture when at last she entered the drawing room.

Aunt Minnie was there before her, seated in a cozy chair drawn close to where Edmond was sitting. He stood as Helen entered the room.

"Good afternoon, Edmond," Helen said in what she gratefully recognized as an even tone. She sat down beside her aunt, saying, "I hope Aunt Minnie has told you how glad we are that you have called upon us."

He resumed his seat, his long legs stretched out before him. "She has, but then, your aunt has always been kind to me."

Minnie touched Helen's hand. "Edmond and I have been reminiscing. Such memories we have! Helen dear, did you know that your mother and Edmond's mother were fast friends? How pleased those dear women would be, I think, to see the two of you together as you are now."

Helen suppressed a groan and wondered if Edmond was as aware as she of her aunt's match-making efforts. "I am certain it is as you say, Aunt Minnie."

"I was just mentioning to Edmond that you and I have decided he must provide you escort to one or two parties and he has agreed. Is that not famous?"

Helen's eyes flew to Edmond's. How much had

Aunt Minnie told him of the humiliating circumstances of her betrothal to Charles? She thought she detected a subtle change in his expression, and she looked away quickly, fearful that she would see that dreaded expression of pity cross his handsome face.

Only moments before she had been delighted by his visit; now she was just as eager to see his visit come to an end before her aunt chose to reveal any other mortifying details about her life. She cudgeled her brain to find some way to steer the conversation to a more neutral topic.

Aunt Minnie saved her the trouble by saying, "I wonder if we may persuade Cook to fix a nice tray of refreshments for us. Why don't I just go see about that?" She was gone from the room before Helen could stop her.

Left alone with Edmond, Helen was suddenly uncomfortable. It had to be as obvious to Edmond as it was to her that Aunt Minnie had deliberately contrived to leave them alone together. To what purpose, she could imagine; to what conclusion Edmond had jumped, she couldn't consider. She couldn't even bring herself to gaze at him, for fear of encountering a look of sympathy or concern that would once again remind her of the humiliating circumstances of her former betrothal.

But as the minutes ticked by, she knew she had to make some attempt at conversation. She said at last, in a constricted voice, "I am certain my aunt will return presently."

"I was rather hoping she would stay away for a while," Edmond said in such a pleasant tone that

Helen's eyes once again flew to his. "It would be a great shame if all her efforts to throw us together came to nothing."

Helen had always prided herself on being a woman of poise, a woman who knew her own worth and could sustain her composure through any test put before her. Edmond Manwaring had brought serious injury to that notion, for yet again, poised, composed Helen found herself blushing in his presence.

She could barely bring herself to look at him as she said, "I fear my aunt has not been very subtle about her intentions. What must you think of us!"

"I think your aunt is a delight. As a matter of fact, I have always thought so."

"But are you not offended by her behavior or embarrassed by her efforts to throw us together?"

He gave his dark head a negligent shake. "Not at all. You and I are merely old friends who have rediscovered each other. It is natural, I think, that we should be on comfortable terms together."

Helen was greatly relieved to hear him say so. "Then you don't mind?"

"How could I when it is clear your aunt only has your welfare at heart?"

"She shall plague you to stand up with me or escort me to parties," Helen warned.

"She only wishes to see you move comfortably in Society again. It would be a shame to disappoint her."

Oddly, Helen wished Edmond had not replied in quite those terms. The knowledge that Edmond might sign his name to her dance card merely to please her aunt inflicted another small bruise upon her already damaged ego.

"What do you say, Helen? Have we a bargain?" He held out his hand toward her. "Shall I be your escort and squire you about for the Season?"

She could have imagined worse ways in which to spend an evening; besides, she rather liked the grown-up version of Edmond Manwaring. Thus far, he had been polite and attentive, and despite a lurking premonition that he might at any moment lapse into a more mature version of the horrid behavior he had exhibited as a child, Helen felt comfortable in his presence.

Impulsively, she placed her fingers in his grasp. "Yes, we have a bargain. But first, before we attend any other parties together, will you allow me one favor? Will you allow me to teach you to dance?"

Edmond regarded her for a moment in stunned silence; then he repeated in an oddly cautious voice, "Teach me to dance? What gave you the impression I was in need of such a lesson?"

"I couldn't help but notice you didn't dance at all last evening, even after Aunt Minnie hinted that she wished you would partner me. I confess, I was at a loss to understand your actions, but then I recalled that as a boy you were—" She hesitated, unsure what, if any, adjective might state her case with the least amount of offense. "Let us merely agree that in your youth, your movements were perhaps less than graceful."

He frowned slightly. "True enough, but that doesn't necessarily mean—"

"No shame attaches to it!" she said quickly. She tightened her fingers, still twined with his, in an encouraging grip. "Let us merely say that dancing is one area of your education that was somehow omitted."

He gave his dark head a slight bewildered shake. "Helen, I shouldn't wish to give you the wrong impression—"

"You mustn't feel that explanations are necessary. Please won't you let me teach you? I daresay that, being such a clever man, you shall be able to learn a simple country dance in very little time."

Edmond looked at Helen a moment in silence; then she saw his lips slant slightly into a half smile that hinted at rueful amusement.

"How can I refuse?" he asked, simply.

She smiled then, feeling almost relieved that he would agree to her scheme. "Shall we begin now?"

His dark brows went up. "Here? In the drawing room?"

"We have only to push a few chairs against the wall. I am certain Aunt Minnie shall not mind, and we needn't fear any embarrassing interruptions," Helen said as she pulled an upholstered chair across the polished floor. She positioned it against the wall and retrieved yet another chair and was grateful when Edmond helped by moving the settee out of the way.

At last, she was satisfied with the amount of floor space they had cleared. "Let us start with a simple country dance," she said. "Here, take my hand."

He did so, and she found he was looking down at her with an odd expression in his eyes she had never seen before. "There's no need to look at me so. If you are worried that others will know about this, I vow that your lesson shall remain our little secret."

One of his dark brows flew questioningly. "Still protecting me, are you, Helen? Do you know, even when you were a girl, your compassionate nature was one of the things I liked most about you."

Perhaps it was the look in his eyes or the low, rather tantalizing manner in which he said those few words, but for some reason, Helen found herself unable to think clearly. She didn't know how to reply and found herself blurting, "But, Edmond, I am not a mere girl any longer."

"No. No, you're not," he said, looking softly down into her eyes.

She had no notion what he meant by such a statement, and for some reason, she was rather fearful of the prospect of finding out. Her heart was beating a good deal faster and her fingers trembled slightly within his grasp. It took a moment for her to come to her senses, but at last she straightened her shoulders and said in a businesslike tone, "Shall we begin the lesson?"

Helen explained to Edmond how he had to stand when first he escorted a lady onto the dance floor; then she went on to describe the various steps of a country dance. Her tone was clear, and her explanations were rational. Yet throughout the lesson, she remained agonizingly conscious of Edmond's hand enfolding hers.

By contrast, Edmond could not have appeared more at ease. He listened carefully to her every instruction and rarely allowed his gaze to wander from her face—a fact that proved sufficient to once again summon an abominable blush to her cheeks.

She took a step and he followed. She instructed him to put his hand to her waist, and he did so, splaying his fingers across her back in a manner that caused her to wish she were teaching him a waltz instead of a *dos-à-dos*. She tensed at the thought and earned from her pupil a kind reminder to watch her steps.

Edmond's first lesson in dancing lasted little more than half an hour for the sole reason that Helen couldn't bear to remain for very much longer in his company. She was unaccustomed to feeling nervous and unsure of her own mind, yet in Edmond's presence, she had been reduced to an unwelcome state of confusion.

Edmond made his good-byes with a slight bow. "I confess, I am looking forward to this evening," he said with a slight smile, which almost convinced her he was capable of reading her thoughts.

Helen drew her hand from his warm grasp, fearful that, if she left it there much longer, she would never wish for him to release it. "So am I," she managed to say, "and please do not be nervous. I am confident you shall make an admirable dance partner."

Edmond was given an opportunity to prove her words correct. Helen and her aunt had been invited to attend a ball, and at Minnie's request, Edmond had agreed to provide his escort. They arrived at the ball just as the dancing was beginning, and no sooner had they laid off their things and greeted their host and hostess than Edmond engaged Helen's hand and led her out onto the dance floor.

Since that afternoon, she had recovered her composure and was determined to behave sensibly in Edmond's presence. "Don't be nervous," she told him encouragingly as the first chords of the dance were struck, "for it is merely a country dance, very much like the one you learned today."

"I'm not nervous," he said, then led her into the first form.

She was on the alert for any misstep or error, for although Edmond had proved to be an exceptional pupil, he had only received a single lesson. She recalled that as a boy he had been much more at ease gamboling across a field than moving with precision across a dance floor. In the end, however, she could find no fault with his performance; rather, he acquitted himself as well, if not better, than any of the other gentlemen present.

Their dance at an end, he drew her over to a rout chair set against the wall and offered to secure her a glass of lemonade. She accepted his offer and was contentedly watching the dancers and patiently awaiting his return when Mrs. Drayton-Kerr came upon her.

She claimed a seat beside Helen, saying in a gush of excitement, "I shall not tarry long for I expect you shall wish me in Jericho once Mr. Manwaring returns. I merely thought to tell you what a splendid couple the two of you made just now. You are to be congratulated."

"Congratulated?" Helen repeated, a little surprised. "Why do you say so?"

"Because of his skill on the dance floor," the lady replied with a knowing smile. "Mr. Manwaring has quite a reputation as an excellent dancer—with good reason, I must say."

Helen frowned slightly. "But Edmond is not an accomplished dancer, ma'am."

"My dear, Mr. Manwaring is much in demand at all the fashionable dance parties and balls this Season. It is said he could dance with a maypole and make it look graceful."

"Edmond?" Helen demanded in disbelief. "But just this afternoon I taught him—" She stopped short and turned to shoot an accusing glance at Edmond as he approached with the promised glass of lemonade.

He looked at her and their eyes met. He smiled slightly—she was certain of it. His lips slanted into that same slight smile he used to flash as a boy that would signal an impending round of teasing.

Helen wrenched her gaze away and said numbly, "It seems I had no idea he was so skilled."

Mrs. Drayton-Kerr smiled. "My dear, I daresay there may be a great number of things we don't know about Mr. Manwaring, but he does have a reputation for being an attentive and skilled dance partner. You could not have selected a more enviable young man to escort you about for the Season." She moved away then, leaving Helen alone and teetering between anger and mortification.

Helen's emotions were not directed at Mrs. Drayton-Kerr, but at Edmond, who reached her side and placed the glass in her hand. He said pleasantly, "Do you think we would set the tongues to wagging if I were to partner you in a second dance?"

There were many things she might have replied, many angry accusations she might have flung in his direction. She was aware, however, that other guests were watching them, and she felt she had no choice but to contain her anger.

"Edmond," she uttered through fairly clenched teeth, "I think you owe me an explanation for your conduct!"

"Now? Could it not wait? Come, there is a new set forming and I think it would do you well to be part of it."

He took the glass from her hand and deposited it on a nearby table. Then he led her out onto the dance floor, saying, "Do you know, when you're angry, you gain a most becoming color in your cheeks. Even as a girl you were never more magnificent than when you were in a fit of pique."

His words only served to anger her more. The music began, and they had made their way through the first pattern of paces before Edmond said, without the least contrition, "I hope you will wait until we have left the ball before you rap me over the thumbs."

At last, his words were enough to fan Helen's irritation into a flame. She hissed in a barely controlled voice, "How little you have changed! I see you still derive enjoyment from the embarrassment of others!"

"It was never my intention to embarrass you, Helen."

"Wasn't it?" she demanded frostily. "You told me you didn't know how to dance!"

"No, *you* said I couldn't dance," he answered dulcetly. "I merely declined to correct you. I learned long ago never to argue with a woman who is intent upon improving me."

The movement of the dance separated them for a few moments, and when they were once again drawn together, he asked, "Are we still friends?"

"It was a wicked trick you played on me," she said, hoping to instill in him a sense of his iniquities.

"A trick that only you and I know about."

"I shall never be peaceful in your company. I shall always wonder what other secrets you have tucked away, ready to reveal at a time calculated to cause me the greatest embarrassment!"

She hadn't expected him to laugh, but he did. His blue eyes sparkled with the light of devilment. "How glad I am to find you have not changed over the years!" he said.

Whether he had meant those words as a compliment or a criticism, she couldn't be sure. She longed to ask him, but once again the dance separated them. Helen stepped a weaving pattern through a row of dancing ladies; she stole a glance at Edmond as he mirrored her steps on the gentlemen's side of the set. He was performing his part with a masculine elegance that was easy to admire. His steps were flawless, and his carriage was graceful, but his eyes were on her.

What he was thinking, she could not guess, but she thought again of his words and couldn't help wondering just how many women there had been who'd felt close enough and comfortable enough with Edmond to try to improve him.

The dance brought them together again and caused Edmond to place his hand at her waist. He could just as well have set a hot iron against her skin, so aware was she of his touch. The slight pressure of his hand at his waist filled her with an odd sense of breathlessness.

She said, with perfect composure, "You have not changed either! And I should not have to remind you what a horrid little boy you were!"

He laughed again, much to Helen's surprise, and took not the least offense at her words. Rather, he seemed to be enjoying himself mightily.

"Drive out with me tomorrow," he invited. At least, she thought it was an invitation, but he spoke the words with such confidence that she wasn't quite sure if she had the power to decline.

She shook her head. "I drive myself in London. I have a phaeton of my own."

"Then take me up in it."

"Why should I?" she demanded, little caring that her words were rude.

"Because I enjoy being with you and I think you feel the same of me if you would but admit it."

The music stopped. Edmond confidently tucked Helen's hand through his arm and guided her to where Aunt Minnie was watching them from the perimeter of the room.

"How splendid the two of you look together!" Minnie said in a twitter of happiness. "Edmond, you must agree to call upon us again tomorrow."

"I believe I have an invitation to drive out with your niece in the morning." He looked down at Helen, one dark brow flying up in question. "Shall I depend upon it?"

Helen meant to scold Edmond; she meant to assure him that she would rather drive a donkey cart with a Newgate prisoner perched beside her than ever drive out with him. But the words didn't come. Instead, she looked up at him and her temper dissolved once again into that curious sensation of breathlessness. His eyes were locked with hers and she detected that hint of devilment lurking in their blue depths, but she also sensed a gentleness there she had not noticed before.

Horrid man! Just when she was well convinced that he was just as infuriating now as he had been ten years before, he cast her a look that sent a ripple of sensation through her. Was it possible that Edmond was correct? *Did* she enjoy being with him?

Helen was still busily trying to sort out her feelings when she heard herself say crossly, "Very well! You may accompany me, but I should warn you that I am a spirited driver!"

"I would have expected nothing less," he said, bowing over her hand. He made his good-byes to Minnie and moved away, but Helen remained vividly aware of his presence in the ballroom.

Several times during the remainder of the evening, she found herself searching him out. Even when she was in conversation with another, Edmond Manwaring remained foremost in her thoughts. Her ears strained to catch the sound of his voice from a distance off; and once, when he ventured close by to engage in conversation with a group of young bucks, Helen was seized by the odd sensation of having her heart flutter in her breast.

From the first moment of reacquainting herself with Edmond Manwaring, Helen had judged him a handsome man. Never had she guessed, however, that his presence could compel her to react in such a manner.

She was unable to account for it and equally unwilling to admit that she felt the least interest in a younger man—one she had known since childhood—who had long enjoyed a well-earned reputation as a hooligan. No, she couldn't possibly be attracted to Edmond Manwaring!

Helen told herself so at least a dozen times that evening, but when at last she was finally in her bed, relaxed and floating in that warm, delicious land between consciousness and sleep, a vision of Edmond's handsome face flitted across her mind. Despite her resolve, despite her protests, Helen Worth fell asleep thinking of Edmond Manwaring.

By the time Edmond called at Worth House the next morning, Helen showed no trace of her previous ill humor toward him. She greeted him amicably, saying as she drew on her driving gloves, "Good morning! I hope the hour is not too early for you."

He held the door open for her to pass through.

"Not at all. I rather like mornings, if the truth be told. I also like you in that habit. Your taste in attire, I notice, remains impeccable."

She allowed him to hand her up into the waiting phaeton and took a moment to settle her skirts about her before taking up the reins. She was dressed in one of her older habits, which was made up of sapphire blue velvet. A tricorn hat, also of velvet and adorned with a slender feather, was set at a jaunty angle atop her curls. It had long been one of her favorite outfits, and she felt a surge of gratification that he would admire it, too.

The phaeton lurched slightly as Edmond climbed up beside her. As soon as he was comfortably settled, she took up her whip.

"Stand away, John!" she commanded of her groom as she snapped her whip with precision at the wheeler's ear. They were off with a burst, and her groom had to scramble for his perch.

Helen drove down the street at a brisk trot. She was a skilled horsewoman and had long been known to drive herself down country lanes or city streets. She set a quick pace and did not slow her horses until they were well within the gates of Hyde Park.

Only then did she dare glance over at Edmond. She had been fully aware of his nearness beside her since the moment he had climbed into the phaeton. Now, as she looked over at his profile, Helen felt an odd suspicion of attraction she dared not recognize. His darkly lashed blue eyes were scanning the passing scenery, and his dark hair ruffled slightly in the breeze. She caught herself wondering how soft his hair might feel if she were to simply reach over and touch it.

She could have slapped herself for such a notion; instead, she tightened her grip on the reins and sought a topic of conversation.

"Have you nothing to say about my driving? Have you no comments to make on my skill with a whip?"

"I admire everything about you, as I always have," he said simply. "And I like the fact that you are much more relaxed now in my presence. When first we were reacquainted, I rather thought that you were on the defensive, that you were steeling yourself against me."

She had never before guessed that Edmond would be so intuitive. Certainly, as a boy, he had never been one to empathize with the discomfort he inflicted on others.

She said carefully, "I suppose I was rather cautious with you. You see, I was afraid you might regard me as an object of pity."

"Why? Because of your betrothal to Addison?" She looked at him quickly, prompting him to say, "Yes, I know about it, and I would gladly call the cur out for having caused that look I see in your eyes. Still, I cannot help but think that sometimes things happen in our lives because they are meant to be. Sometimes adversity can work out well in the end."

She found little comfort in his words, but said unconvincingly, "I suppose you may be right."

He laughed. "Don't ever try to lie to me. You have no talent for it!"

"I hope I may be relied upon to always speak the

truth," she said primly, not knowing how else to respond.

"That," he said, "is another thing about you that hasn't changed over the years. And yet, there is a difference in you. You are much more on your guard now, I think. You used to be possessed of enough confidence for two men. You never used to care what others thought of you."

"That was before I realized that I could be the object of pity. Oh, I know I never loved Charles Addison, and I cannot bemoan the fact that I shall not spend the rest of my life with him. But, Edmond, you have no notion what it is like to enter a room and know that people you once counted as friends are whispering about you behind their hands! It was all so mortifying!"

"Why?"

"Can you not guess? To be a spinster by choice is one thing. To be handed my congé by a man who once said he wanted to marry me is something altogether different!"

Edmond was quiet a moment, watching the passing scenery as they began to tour the park for a second time. "Pull up over there," he said abruptly, pointing toward the grove of trees on the west end of the park. "At this hour of the morning, we have the entire park to ourselves. It would be a shame to waste it. Walk with me awhile."

She did as he asked and waited for John Groom to run to the leader's head before she allowed Edmond to assist her down. He drew her gloved hand through his arm and led her toward the grove.

Glancing up at Edmond, Helen briefly studied the features of his face: the vividness of his eyes; the strong, forceful planes of his face; the humor and intelligence of his lively countenance. Unlike the day before, when she had been nervous and uncertain with Edmond, Helen now felt altogether comforted in his presence, as if she were simply strolling through the park with an old, dear, and trusted friend.

She smiled slightly at a long-ago memory. "I do not think I should walk any farther with you. The last time we were in a grove together such as this, you tied me to a tree and threatened to put an apple on my head. You claimed at the time to be a great admirer of William Tell!"

He smiled, revealing a row of even white teeth. "Was I very horrid to you?"

"Barbarous!"

He laughed. "If it's any comfort to you, I didn't really want to shoot an apple from your head. What I really wanted to do was kiss you, but I couldn't summon the courage."

She couldn't have been more surprised if he had doused her with a bucket of water. She stopped walking, and her eyes flew to his. Their gazes locked; his glance was calm and even, while hers held the same startled quality of a doe surprised alone in a clearing.

They stood thus only a moment; then Edmond placed his hand over hers, as it rested on his arm, and drew her forward again. The light pressure of his hand and the memory of the manner in which he had looked at her filled Helen with an odd sense of wonder. She found it difficult to take a deep, controlling breath, then found it even harder to consider any coherent thought but that Edmond wanted to kiss her. She was as certain of it as she was of her own name. Even more certainly, she wanted to kiss him back.

It was an astonishing thought, and for a moment, she considered the possibility that she might actually be losing her mind. Did she truly feel a desire to kiss Edmond Manwaring, the former Evil Edmond, terror of Derbyshire?

Abruptly, she stopped walking. "I must return home. I promised Aunt Minnie I would pay morning calls with her. She must not be disappointed!"

"No, she musn't. Come, I'll take you back."

Edmond climbed up in the phaeton after Helen and sat down close beside her—disturbingly close, she realized. Her senses were filled with him: the scent of his leather gloves, the masculine aroma of his cologne; the warm, musky fragrance of his wool coat. She was vividly conscious of everything about him as they drove back to Worth House.

Edmond declined to come inside with Helen, but bade her a good day at the door. She didn't know whether to be relieved or disappointed that he made no move to bring her hand to his lips or to boldly kiss her on the step.

Yet when she went into the house, she floated up the stairs and down the hall to her bedchamber just as if he had indeed kissed her soundly upon the lips.

How long she remained in her room, lost in the memory of her time with Edmond, she had no idea. A maid knocked at her door to announce that luncheon was being served. Helen's normally healthy appetite had long since vanished.

So, she judged, had her reasoning, for she suddenly realized that Edmond must have noticed her behavior. He must have noticed how foolishly she had gaped at him and failed on their drive back to put even two sensible words together in a simple sentence. She wondered, too, if he'd noticed that she was teetering very near the brink of falling in love with him.

It could not be.

Countless times, Helen repeated the words silently to herself.

"It cannot be!" she said aloud. Edmond was the root of every horrid childhood memory. Yet some illogical place deep within her heart betrayed her with a spark of affection for Edmond Manwaring.

The next afternoon, with a maid to accompany her, Helen ventured out to the shops. Her aunt, hearing of her proposed excursion, charged her with several errands. Helen had just completed the last of these when she heard her name called.

Turning, she saw Edmond driving a well-sprung curricle up the street toward her. Since the morning before, when he had returned her to Worth House after their drive in the park, Helen's thoughts had never strayed far from Edmond. In the privacy of her own bedchamber, it had been an easy task to convince herself that she felt not the least emotion where he was concerned. Now, standing in the hub of Bond

Street, Helen felt as if her heart were about to rise in her throat at the very sight of him.

He drew up beside her and touched his gloved fingers to the brim of his hat. "Good day! I was hoping I might see you again before this evening."

She looked up at him, a question in her eyes. "This evening?"

"Yes. Your aunt sent round a note to me yesterday afternoon, saying you were in need of my escort tonight at Lady Mayberry's musicale. I was just driving over to assure her she could count on me."

Helen almost groaned out loud, but stopped herself in time. Aunt Minnie! Helen would have a few choice words to say to her dear aunt as soon as she returned home.

Edmond moved over to one side of the curricle. "Are you done with your errands? Let me take you to your door." He reached down his hand to her.

Despite her better judgment, despite the many reasons she knew she should decline, in the end, no force on earth could have kept Helen from scrambling up into that curricle. She hoped, at least, that she did so with sufficient grace that Edmond did not suspect how happy she was to find herself once again by his side.

He took up his reins and commanded his groom to see Helen's maid home. "I shall meet you at Worth House, Thomas," he said, then set his curricle in motion.

He was silent for a few minutes as he negotiated the city traffic. At last, he said conversationally, "I have had a letter from my father. He writes of all the news at home and keeps me abreast of all the gossip.''

Helen laughed. ''His letters must be brief, for there is never any news of great import from our little neighborhood in Derbyshire.''

Edmond smiled slightly. ''You're right, of course. His letters never contain any news more exciting than crop yields and new foals. At his most exciting, he writes of nothing more noteworthy than a betrothal or the birth of a baby.''

''I daresay he writes because he misses you. No doubt the Manwaring estate is much quieter since you have come to London.''

Edmond had been minding his horses, but at that remark, he directed a quick glance of surprise at her. ''Indeed? Why do you say so?''

''Who else is left in Derbyshire to create mischief and mayhem in the same manner you did? You were forever stirring up one bit of trouble after another, as I recall.''

''Helen, you are recounting the deeds and follies I committed as a boy,'' he said with a slight frown. ''In case you haven't noticed, I'm a grown man now.''

''I had noticed,'' she said, feeling suddenly uncomfortable.

''Have you? Then why do I have the distinct impression that you fully expect me at any moment to engage in the sort of tricks and deviltry I used to in my youth?''

Helen thought she detected a hint of exasperation in his tone and said, somewhat defensively, ''I cannot help myself, Edmond. I know I should not, but when I look at you, I see the boy I knew ten years ago.''

He cast her a grim look and uttered a muffled sound that Helen could not quite categorize. They were traveling down the street toward Worth House, but abruptly, without so much as a warning, Edmond altered their course. With a practiced skill, he sent his team of horses flying around the next corner to the square, where he drew the curricle to an unexpected halt. There, hidden on one side by the ivy-covered gate, Edmond wrapped his arm about Helen's shoulders and pulled her to him. His head bent over hers and his lips met her own.

She started at his touch and instinctively tried to draw back, but his fingers twined in her hair and he held her securely, allowing no possibility of escape.

Not that she considered escaping, for no sooner had her brain recognized that she was being kissed than her body began to betray her. A delicious warmth sprang to life deep within her and began to slowly spread through her limbs like melted wax. His lips teased hers until she thought she could stand no more; then he kissed her soundly, sweetly, until she wished that his kiss might never end.

It did, much too soon for her satisfaction. He raised his head slightly and looked at her. "Well? Now do you see me as a grown man, Helen Worth?" he demanded.

Her lips were still tingling and her mind was still muddled from the effects of his kisses, but she managed to say, with a good deal of confusion, "You just kissed me on a public street!"

"Yes, I did. And I'll kiss you a hundred times more if that's what it will take to make you see me as I am, rather than what I once was."

Edmond straightened slightly and pulled his arm from about her shoulders. Recklessly, Helen wished he would put it back and hold her again. She wished he would look down upon her again with the same mixture of tenderness, mischief, and desire she had seen in his blue eyes only moments ago. Instead, she blurted, "You didn't have to kiss me to prove your point."

"Yes, I did," he countered grimly as he took up the reins and set the curricle in motion again. "You were in need of some shaking up, Helen Worth."

She couldn't decide what he meant by such a statement. She thought he might have meant to insult her, but discarded the notion when she realized that his words made a good deal more sense than she had previously thought.

Edmond was right. She had been thinking of him as nothing more than a larger version of the rascal she had known as a little boy. She was wrong to have done so, but said, by way of excusing herself, "I suppose you are right. I have been thinking of you in terms of my memory. But in my defense, I really don't know anything about you, do I?"

Edmond looked down at Helen appraisingly. "I shall gladly tell you about myself. You have only to ask."

"I wouldn't know where to begin," she said.

"Only tell me what you wish to know."

There were many things she might have asked him,

many things she should have learned, but without thinking, without even considering her words, she blurted, "Have you any attachments?"

The words were out before she could consider them, and so embarrassed was she by her own lack of finesse, she could have crawled under the curricle seat.

His dark brows came together beneath the brim of his hat. "Attachments? Do you mean my family?"

"No, not exactly," she replied, feeling wretchedly self-conscious. She wished she had never asked the question, but reasoned that as long as the subject was broached, she might as well plunge forward. "I was more interested to know if you were, perhaps, betrothed or attached to any particular lady of your acquaintance. You spoke so knowledgeably to me before of marriage engagements," she added in weak explanation.

"No," he said gently. "I am not betrothed, although I have from time to time given the matter a good deal of consideration. Let us merely say that I have an understanding."

Good heavens, Helen thought, *what does that mean?*

"An understanding?" she repeated.

"Yes. Some time ago, I made a pact with a woman whose judgment I value."

Helen felt her heart sink all the way to her shoes. A sudden vision leapt to her mind of Edmond, impeccably dressed, dancing across a ballroom with a beautiful woman in his arms—a woman younger than Helen, a woman who had no memory of the high jinks Edmond had committed as a boy.

She looked over at him and was suddenly resentful of his handsome face, of his alluring smile, of the dancing lights of amusement in his blue eyes. How dared he make her feel such an attraction to him!

"I am glad to hear it," she said, striving to keep her voice light. "I hope you shall be very happy with her."

Edmond drew his horses to a stop in front of Worth House and looked at Helen, a question in his blue eyes. "Happy with her?" he repeated.

"Yes. I wish you well, Edmond. After all, we are friends, are we not?" she said and was amazed to discover how easily such hated words sprang from her lips. She was feeling utterly miserable by the time she entered the house. She wished for nothing more than the quiet solace of her room, where she might throw herself on the bed and engage in a fit of weeping.

That prospect was denied her when Minnie emerged from the library, a book in her hand. She turned and asked curiously, "My dear, where is your maid?"

"On Bond Street. I left her there. Edmond Manwaring drove me home in his curricle."

There was no mistaking the smile of pleasure that crossed her aunt's face. "Did he? How splendid! But, my dear, why did you not invite him in? Of all things, you should never have left him at the door!"

"I should never have met him again," Helen said wretchedly. Her chin began to quiver slightly. "I should never have allowed him to escort me to parties. And I should never have fallen in love with him!"

Minnie's eyes widened; the book fell unnoticed to the floor. "My dear!"

Minnie drew Helen into the library and guided her toward the nearest chair. Helen sank down upon it slowly, and without so much as a sob, the first tear left her eye and coursed slowly down her cheek.

"My dear child, why are you crying? You have fallen in love with Edmond Manwaring! I should think that excellent cause for happiness, not tears!"

With trembling fingers, Helen untied the ribbons of her bonnet from beneath her chin and set the bonnet on a nearby chair. "Aunt, I cannot be happy when Edmond is betrothed to another."

"Betrothed?" Minnie repeated, her attention arrested. "He could not be. I am certain of it!"

"He told me less than two minutes ago that he had an understanding with a woman. He said he valued her judgment."

"That sounds most peculiar, my dear," Minnie said after a moment's consideration. "Did he say nothing of love?"

Love! That wretched word! Helen felt as if a little piece of her heart were about to break off. "Oh, Aunt! I have been such a fool!" she uttered as her tears began to flow more freely. "I've fallen in love with a man who could not be more dissimilar from myself. He's younger than I, practically betrothed to another, and no more interested in me than a brother would be. Oh, what a mull I have made of it!"

Minnie quickly wrapped a consoling arm about Helen's shoulders and pressed an embroidered kerchief into her hand. "I can scarcely believe it! Helen, there must be something you have misunderstood. I am well convinced Edmond cares for you."

"He has never said so. In fact, he has on more than one occasion said that we were merely friends. Why, once he said we were as brother and sister. I should have listened! I should have heeded his words. But I was so busy marveling over the changes in him that I was in love with him before I even realized!"

"Helen dearest, you mustn't carry on so," her aunt said bracingly. "I have heard myself the way he compliments you. He cares for you, I think, more than you know."

"Cares for me? At the same time, he is almost betrothed to another woman? That behavior, I assure you, is worse than any he ever exhibited as a boy!"

Minnie frowned, concern clearly written upon her face. "My dear, I beg you to reconsider! If only—"

"Dearest Aunt, you cannot suppose for one moment that, no matter what my feelings, I would ever consider coming between a man and a woman who are bound for marriage. Not after all that I have been through! I could never bring myself to do such a thing!"

"But, dear, if Edmond loves you—"

"It doesn't signify," Helen said firmly. "Whether he loves me or not, I could never be a party to the end of another woman's engagement. I thought that you, of all people, would understand!"

It was clear from the expression on Minnie's face that she was not at all in agreement with her niece, but she had learned long ago that Helen was possessed of a good deal of willfulness. Once Helen made up her mind in a matter, and knew herself to be in the right, she rarely veered from her chosen path.

That willfulness and sense of purpose were all the armor Helen had about her when she met Edmond later that evening. Aunt Minnie, in her latest attempt to throw them together, had cried off escorting Helen to a musicale that had long been on their schedule. She had begged Edmond to take her place and escort Helen in her stead, and she was very well pleased when he accepted.

Edmond arrived at the appointed hour and was ushered into the drawing room, only to find that Helen was there before him, nervously pacing the floor.

She turned abruptly when he entered the room and clasped her hands together in a tight grip of control. It was most unfair, she thought bitterly, that Edmond Manwaring should be so attractive. When he was near her, she felt herself drawn to him in an almost magnetic way; when they were apart, a vision of his handsome face and a memory of every word he had ever spoken to her spun about her brain.

He was dressed rather formally in coat and breeches that showed his muscular body to advantage. He smiled when he saw her, and his eyes met hers for a long, lingering moment. Then, his gaze shifted and traveled over the thin fabric of her afternoon gown.

He frowned slightly in puzzlement. "Helen? Why aren't you dressed?"

"I hope you won't mind if we don't go out this evening. You see, I have something to say to you."

He smiled slightly. "I can think of no better way to

pass the evening than to spend it here in conversation with you.''

There was a fire burning low in the grate. He went over to it and nudged the toe of his shoe against a log. The log shifted and the fire sprang to life, sending a golden glow of light across the room.

"That's better,'' he said with satisfaction. Then he cast her a look that immediately set her on her guard. "What is it you wish to talk about? No, let me guess! You want to talk about this afternoon.''

She drew a deep breath and said with surprising composure, "That is exactly what I wish to speak to you about.''

"More specifically, I would hazard a guess that you want to talk about our kiss.'' He took a few steps toward her.

Helen felt as if her heart had begun to thump wildly in her breast and she couldn't decide if she was more alarmed by his words or his slow advancement upon her. "No! No, not at all!''

"No? What then? What do you wish to say to me, Helen?''

Mulishly, she put up her chin and said, "I wish to tell you that I cannot see you, Edmond. I should prefer it if you did not call at Worth House again.''

He was so surprised by her words that he could only stare at her, thunderstruck. *"What?* Helen, what are you talking about?''

"I am speaking of your . . . your—'' She couldn't bring herself to speak of marriage, while her heart was breaking. "Of the arrangement you mentioned.''

"What arrangement?" he demanded and took a step toward her.

"Please don't make this difficult, Edmond. I have given this matter no small amount of thought, and I find I cannot allow our relationship to go further."

"Our relationship, as you put it, has only begun. Why are you so eager to toss it aside?"

"I am not eager," she protested, losing a good deal of her self-control. "Oh, Edmond, don't you understand? Having been the victim of a man with a fickle heart myself, I have all the sympathy in the world for the other young lady involved. Why, I could never bring myself to cause another woman the same pain I was made to suffer when Charles Addison broke off our betrothal! Please don't ask me to be a party to this! I refuse to come between you and your fiancée."

His brows came together and he had a look about him of promised thunder. "My fiancée?" he repeated. "Helen, just which fiancée exactly are you talking about?"

His question threw her off guard. "How many do you have?" she demanded, thinking it an inopportune time for Edmond to revert to the horrid way he'd had of teasing her when he was a child.

"I haven't any fiancée at all, Helen," he replied quite calmly, and to her dismay, he took yet another few steps in her direction.

"But you said you had an understanding! You told me there was a woman whose judgment you valued!"

"Indeed, there was. Someone I often turned to for advice and guidance. Helen, the lady was my mother."

She looked up at him stupidly. He was still advancing upon her, still watching her with that familiar light of devilment in his blue eyes.

"Your mother?"

"Yes. She taught me long ago that, if I want to be truly happy in life, I must marry for love."

Edmond closed the last of the distance between them and was standing so close upon Helen that she caught the faint aroma of his cologne. His nearness was seriously impairing her ability to think clearly, but she managed to say, "But you mentioned an understanding."

"True—an understanding with my mother. Before she died, she and I struck a bargain. It sustained me through the difficult times when she was gone from me. We made a promise, and since I was young and missed her dreadfully, I believed she would keep her part, so I had no choice but to keep mine."

"What was the bargain?"

"My mother made me promise that I would not marry any woman who did not love me truly, madly, and deeply. For her part, she made me a promise that from her seat in heaven, she would scour the land until she found the right girl for me, and when the time was right, she would lead me to her." He smiled slightly. "As a boy, it was comforting to think that my mother was watching over me. As a young man full of worldly doubts, I thought the prospect of my mother watching me from heaven was rather absurd."

"And now?"

"And now, as a grown man, I cannot help but believe that she led me straight to you."

Helen said thoughtfully, "Your mother and my mother were fast friends. Aunt Minnie told me so."

"I think your mother and mine conspired long ago that we should make a match of it." His hand cupped her chin, sending tremors of sensation through her. "It seems that we were destined for each other. You can't fight destiny, Helen."

She felt her whole body relax. All the tension, all the pent-up emotion that had plagued her throughout the day, disappeared with the simple touch of his hand on her face. "I wouldn't dream of trying," she said softly.

Edmond's arms reached out and he drew her to him. His cheek brushed against the top of her curls for a moment; then his fingers gently brought her chin up until she was looking into his eyes.

He dipped his head, and his lips moved tenderly across her forehead, then teasingly trailed across her cheekbone. At last, his lips met hers in a warm, deep kiss.

Without even considering, Helen clung to his lapel and reveled in the feel of his arms about her. Sweetness and wildfire mingled in his kiss, and just as she began to wish that it would go on forever, he raised his head.

"My beautiful Helen," he murmured. "I've loved you for so long."

True happiness bubbled inside her. "You have? But I had no idea, for you were always so horrid. I often wondered why you behaved the way you did."

"I did it to get your attention."

She gave a slight, uncertain laugh. "Why would you wish to do that?"

"Because you were beautiful. Because I was a little bit in love with you even as a boy, but you were older and much more grown-up and sophisticated. Terrorizing you was my way of making you notice me, I think."

"Edmond, I had no idea you felt that way," she said, slightly stunned.

"I know. But I've grown up and over the years I learned better ways to attract a woman's attention."

He certainly had Helen's attention. In fact, she was having a difficult time thinking of anything but the fact that he was holding her close and that his lips remained tantalizingly close to hers.

His hand touched her cheek in a tender, brief caress; then he teasingly brushed his lips again over hers.

Helen felt as if her nerves had caught on fire. She responded without thinking, reaching up to draw Edmond even closer, to invite him to deepen his kiss.

After a few moments of such sweet madness, he abruptly raised his head. "I think that's enough for now," he said, his voice sounding a trifle shaky. "As tempting as you are and as much as I wish to show you just how much I love you, we aren't even formally betrothed, let alone married."

"Then let us be betrothed," she said eagerly.

A light danced to life in his blue eyes. "Are you certain, Helen? You'll marry me?"

She nodded vigorously. "Of course!"

"Are you very sure? I'm younger than you, you know. And I have a wicked sense of humor, as you have reminded me on many occasions."

"I should never have said such things to you, for they don't signify!"

"When?" he demanded. "When will you marry me?"

Helen gave his question only the briefest consideration. "What would you say if I were to tell you that I already have a new trousseau hanging in my wardrobe? What would you think if I said that a wedding breakfast is already planned for a lovely day in June less than two weeks away?"

"I should say that I love you, Helen Worth," Edmond said, taking her a little roughly into his arms and holding her securely, as if he thought she might try to escape. "And while I might have to wait to marry you, I intend to begin right now proving that I do indeed love you truly, madly, and deeply."

ABOUT THE AUTHOR

Nancy Lawrence lives with her family in Aurora, CO. She is the author of five Zebra Regency romances: *Delightful Deception, A Scandalous Season, Once Upon a Christmas, A Noble Rogue,* and *Miss Hamilton's Hero.* Her newest Zebra Regency romance, *An Intimate Arrangement* will be published in January 2000. Nancy loves hearing from her readers and you may write to her c/o Zebra Books. Please include a self-addressed stamped envelope if you wish a response.

YOU WON'T WANT TO READ
JUST ONE—KATHERINE STONE

ROOMMATES   (0-8217-5206-5, $6.99/$7.99)
No one could have prepared Carrie for the monumental
changes she would face when she met her new circle of friends
at Stanford University. Once their lives intertwined and became
woven into the tapestry of the times, they would never be the
same.

TWINS   (0-8217-5207-3, $6.99/$7.99)
Brook and Melanie Chandler were so different, it was hard to
believe they were sisters. One was a dark, serious, ambitious
New York attorney; the other, a golden, glamourous, sophisticated supermodel. But they were more than sisters—they were
twins and more alike than even they knew . . .

THE CARLTON CLUB   (0-8217-5204-9, $6.99/$7.99)
It was the place to see and be seen, the only place to be. And
for those who frequented the playground of the very rich, it
was a way of life. Mark, Kathleen, Leslie and Janet—they
worked together, played together, and loved together, all behind
exclusive gates of the *Carlton Club.*

*Available wherever paperbacks are sold, or order direct from the
Publisher. Send cover price plus 50¢ per copy for mailing and
handling to Kensington Publishing Corp., Consumer Orders,
or call (toll free) 888-345-BOOK, to place your order using
Mastercard or Visa. Residents of New York and Tennessee
must include sales tax. DO NOT SEND CASH.*

LOOK FOR THESE REGENCY ROMANCES